FOR THE LOVE OF A BOSS 2

C.D. Blue

Lock Down Publications and Ca$h
Presents
FOR THE LOVE OF A BOSS 2
A Novel by *C.D. Blue*

C.D. Blue

Lock Down Publications
P.O. Box 944
Stockbridge, Ga 30281
www.lockdownpublications.com

Copyright 2021 C.D. Blue
For the Love of a Boss 2

First Edition July 2021
Printed in the United States of America

This is a work of fiction. Names, characters, places, and incidents either are products of the author's imagination or are used fictitiously. Any similarity to actual events or locales or persons, living or dead, is entirely coincidental.

Lock Down Publications
Like our page on Facebook: Lock Down Publications @
www.facebook.com/lockdownpublications.ldp

Book interior design by: **Shawn Walker**
Edited by: **Nuel Uyi**

4

Stay Connected with Us!

Text **LOCKDOWN** to 22828 to stay up-to-date with new
releases, sneak peaks, contests and more…
Thank you!

Submission Guideline.

Submit the first three chapters of your completed manuscript to ldpsubmissions@gmail.com, subject line: Your book's title. The manuscript must be in a .doc file and sent as an attachment. Document should be in Times New Roman, double spaced and in size 12 font. Also, provide your synopsis and full contact information. If sending multiple submissions, they must each be in a separate email.

Have a story but no way to send it electronically? You can still submit to LDP/Ca$h Presents. Send in the first three chapters, written or typed, of your completed manuscript to:

LDP: Submissions Dept
P.O. Box 944
Stockbridge, Ga 30281

DO NOT send original manuscript. Must be a duplicate.

Provide your synopsis and a cover letter containing your full contact information.

Thanks for considering LDP and Ca$h Presents.

Acknowledgements

Thanking God first as always for giving me the visions to create my stories. My family, of course, I wouldn't be able to make it without the love and support you guys give. I can't forget my day ones: Calandra, Jennifer, Peggy, and Amber, thanks for your support and all of the readers you introduced my work to. I will always appreciate you! One of the best perks of my writing career is the lifetime friendships I've gained.

Thank you readers! I mean, what is a book without readers? I'm glad you enjoy my work and there is more to come. As long as I write, I hope you will read.

Every book contains a piece of me, but this particular series holds bigger portions than most. I have to thank the people who made this story come to life. Memories last forever.

Thanking the LDP family for welcoming into the circle. I appreciate the love. A special thanks to LDP CEO CA$H, you have my utmost respect and admiration always.

C.D. Blue

C.D. Blue

Chapter One

"Tee?" he heard her whisper.

There was nothing for him to hold and he was scared if he touched her it would hurt her.

"I'm here, Zan," he told her softly.

Tears ran down her face. She said something, but it was so low he couldn't hear her.

"What'd you say?"

"Sorry," came the garbled reply.

That hit him like a ton of bricks! There was the answer about his baby. Damn!

"It's alright, we'll have another one, I promise." Seeing her like that made him forget that not only had he been about to break up with her, but also that he said he didn't want to be tied to her for a long time.

It looked like she tried to smile, so he threw in his own joke.

"But next time you won't be wearing no heels," he chuckled.

Once again, she said something he couldn't hear.

"What was that?"

His whole world shattered at her words.

"Lissa did this. She pushed me."

Taj shook his head, clearly he hadn't heard right. "What?"

"Kalissa pushed me down the stairs." Zandra's words were slurred, and tears ran down her face.

With narrowing eyes Taj relived the scene—how Kalissa had run down behind Zandra, covering her mouth, how Kalissa paced, but never shed a tear while they waited for the ambulance, and how much she hated Zandra.

Before he could respond, Mr. Banks roared back into the small area.

"Okay, your two minutes are up! Look at what you did! Got her all upset, get the hell out of here now!"

Mr. Banks reached for Taj, but stepped back when Taj threw him a look of pure hate.

"I'll be back later, Zan, I promise."

9

Mrs. Banks threw him a pitiful smile as he stormed past her, heading to the waiting area. Once the automatic door opened, he stomped through and paused to take a deep breath. Within the few minutes he had been in the back, the waiting room had become crowded, or maybe he just hadn't noticed. Taj spotted Nigel and Kalissa, as he scanned the roomful of people.

Nigel and Kalissa sat in the back corner. Nigel was sprawled in the uncomfortable looking chair, seemingly asleep, while Kalissa sat with a disturbed look on her face. Ever since they had been kids, she got that look when something was bothering her; Taj knew it well.

As he headed their way, Kalissa spotted him and stood, replacing her bothered look with a look of concern. Once Taj noticed that, he forgot about hearing her side of the story. He knew her concern was fake.

When he got closer to them, Kalissa stepped forward and grabbed his arm.

"How is—" Kalissa began.

"What did you do, Lissa?"

"What?" Confusion lined her face,

"What the hell did you do?" Taj raised his voice.

"What are you talking about, Taj?" Kalissa asked in a stage whisper, looking around.

Taj followed her lead and lowered his voice, slightly. "You know exactly what I'm talking about! You pushed Zandra down the stairs!"

Kalissa looked shocked, released his arm, then with a slight chuckle, said, "Where did you get that crazy idea from?"

Something about her finding it funny set him off. "I got it from Zandra! Do you have any fucking idea what you did?"

"Hol' up, mane. Who the fuck you think you talking to?" Nigel stood, mean mugging Taj.

"This ain't got shit to do wit' you, nigga," Taj stood his ground.

"I ain't yo' nigga and you need to lower yo' muthafuckin' tone," Nigel said, as he stepped between Taj and Kalissa.

10

Kalissa moved in front of Nigel, keeping a hand on his arm. "Taj, Zandra told you that I pushed her? And you believe her? I did not push her!"

"Why would she lie, Lissa? Huh? Why the fuck would she lie about something like that?"

Lissa looked at him with a pinched face, her nostrils flared.

"Because she is a fucking liar, that's why!"

"She's under too much medication to come up wit' some lie jus' to be lying. Nah, I ain't buying that," Taj said as he shook his head.

The people in the waiting room were enjoying the show, and the security guard at the door stood at attention, waiting for something to go down. Kalissa looked around, taking it all in, before stepping closer to her friend.

"I can't stop you from believing what you want. All I can tell you is that when I saw her wobbling, I tried to grab her to stop her from falling. I thought her heel had gotten stuck or something. But Tee, man, you know me. Why would you come at me with some bullshit like this? If you think I would push her, then you really don't know me at all."

They stood glaring at each other. Taj noticed the flecks of green in her unwavering eyes, while Kalissa saw the hurt and anger in his.

Frowning, Taj said: "I thought I did, but now I don't know. Nah, you pushing her down the stairs made her lose our baby, Lissa. You can't make me believe that Zan would lie about that! Hell naw!"

Lissa stepped back in shock but held her ground. "Come on, Tee, you know that ain't me. Come on now." Tears had gathered in her eyes, and her voice shook with emotion.

Taj's anger had him in such a tizzy he never noticed her tears. "Nah, ain't no way she lying 'bout this! If she had just fell and it was an accident, that's all it is. But you trying to tell me that she's lying about how she lost our baby?" He shook his head vehemently. "Nah, man, nobody would do that. You killed my baby, Lissa! How could you do that, man?"

Kalissa wrapped her arms around her stomach as if she had been punched, then her eyes turned cold. "I hate you lost yo' baby, but I didn't do anything, Tee. But I also see that nothing I say will make you believe me."

Kalissa turned and walked away, while Nigel mean mugged him for a second before bumping into Taj's shoulder as he followed her.

***

The dashboard lights illuminated the small space of Nigel's BMW. They rode in silence until the first light caught them on the boulevard.

The lights reflected off the windows, as Kalissa stared and thought about what had just happened. Anger filtered through her body, as she thought about how scared she had been for Zandra. Just for that bitch to turn around and lie against her! On the flip side, she felt the pain from Taj's words. His accusations and the hate she heard in his voice cut her like a knife. There was no reason that he should have ever believed that she would do something like that, unless he had always thought of her that way. That thought alone brought a new wave of hurt.

"You a'ight, lil' mama?"

Kalissa nodded silently, continuing to look out of the window. When she spoke, the corners of her mouth trembled, and her voice shook. "I'm tired. It's been a rough day."

His hand reached out and stroked her thigh; the feeling was weirdly comforting and annoying at the same time.

"Lil' mama, don't worry about what them niggas think. You know you didn't do nothing, so fuck them! I mean, you didn't push her down the stairs, did you?"

Kalissa snapped her head around to look at him. "You are asking me that for real?"

"Aye, it never crossed my mind until he came wit' that bull-shit. I don't care if you did, I just can't figure out why she would say that,"

"Nah, I didn't push her." Sucking her teeth, she finished quietly, "She said that because that bitch hates me. I don't fool wit' her, but I don't hate her. Sometimes it seems as if all my life, either I'm invisible or people dislike me. I don't know what's wrong with me."

"Baby, believe me, people notice you. And the ones that don't like you, fuck them, you don't need them anyway." Nigel squeezed her thigh and glanced over at her, but Lissa continued looking out the window.

Nigel tried to think of something else to say but before he could open his mouth, Kalissa's phone rang, interrupting them. It was Fefe.

"Hey, girl," Kalissa answered, sounding tired.

"Where y'all at? I been calling everybody and nobody's answering the phone," Fefe sounded energized.

"I'm headed home. Zandra fell down the stairs and we're leaving the hospital now."

"What! Is she alright? Oh my God!" Fefe yelled.

"Yeah, she's okay, obviously. She's still in the emergency room."

"Girl, I'll meet you at yo' place. I ain't coming to the hospital tipsy," Fefe said before hanging up.

Fefe must have been close because when they pulled up, she was peeping into Lissa's car. She shielded her eyes with her hand when they pulled up.

"Hey! I thought you were by yourself," Fefe said when Lissa stepped out of Nigel's car.

For some reason that rubbed Kalissa the wrong way, she had a gut feeling that something was off, especially as she recalled what Zandra had told her concerning Fefe and Nigel, but she'd dismissed it as one of the lies Zandra told, so she kept her mouth in check. Somewhat.

"I don't know why you thought that. I wasn't alone when you saw me a lil' while ago."

"Girl, I was just saying, no need to jump down my throat," Fefe snapped. She turned towards Nigel. "Hey, Nigel." Fefe led them up the stairs as if she lived there.

Nigel opened the door, letting the women in.

"Ump, you got a key now?" Fefe said before they made it in good.

"Fe! Shut yo' damn trap, mane, damn!" Nigel yelled.

Kalissa got a bad vibe, and her intuition was telling her something she did not want to hear. With Desi's funeral, Zandra's fall and Taj not believing her, she couldn't deal with her intuition. She decided to ignore it.

Nigel turned on the television, and sat on the sofa with his legs splayed apart. "Lissa, get me a beer. Please."

Trying to shake the bad energy and the hurt that still fit her like a glove, she rolled her eyes playfully and stomped to the kitchen. Once in the kitchen, she felt foolish because she knew her moves came off more goofy than playful. The one thing she hated more than anything was, trying to act okay when internally she was falling apart. That routine had become so commonplace with her, she didn't know any other way. Before she opened the fridge, something shiny under the stove caught her eye. Kneeling down, she realized it was an earring she thought she'd lost. It probably fell off the night she and Nigel got busy in the kitchen.

That memory made a true smile cross her face. Nigel's words in the car hadn't helped much because she felt as if he was just saying something to make her feel better. Him rubbing her back and showing her his love would definitely make her feel better. Fefe needed to go home quickly. Instead of one beer, she grabbed two and closed the fridge with her foot. A giggle from the living room sent a cold chill down her spine.

The only memory that crossed her mind when she walked out of the kitchen was Zandra's cruel words. Fefe sat next to Nigel with her tits laying on his arm as he showed her something on his phone. Their body language was too familiar, and it made Zandra's words not just hurtful, but plausible. Fefe's fake, flirtatious giggles increased until Kalissa slid Nigel's beer on the coffee table. Fefe moved slightly back, enough for her titties to get off Nigel's arm.

Taking a long sip out of her bottle while she processed the scene in front of her, narrowing her eyes as the liquid went down, Kalissa popped her lips.

"So, when was I supposed to find out that y'all been fucking?"

C.D. Blue

Chapter Two

Taj was torn between leaving the hospital and staying until Zandra got admitted. In a moment of honesty, he knew that the altercation with Lissa had him more upset than anything else. *Why the hell would she have pushed Zandra down cement stairs?*

Immediately after that thought, he heard Zandra's words about how he always put Kalissa before her, and Taj realized she was right. No matter what flaws Zandra had, he hadn't treated her like he should have, especially after she told him she was pregnant.

With his mind made up to go back with Zandra, regardless of how her dad acted, Taj began walking towards the automated doors. Before he could reach it, he saw Mrs. Banks walk out, looking around until she spotted him. Taj met her halfway.

Mrs. Banks led him around the corner, away from the people in the waiting room.

"I'm so glad I caught you before you left. Please just ignore the mister, he's just upset. I mean, first it was the miscarriage, now this. It didn't help that he never even knew Zan was pregnant." Mrs. Banks wrung her hands while she spoke.

Her words bounced around in Taj's head. "Miscarriage?" Taj repeated the word to make sure he heard her correctly.

"Oh, I'm sorry, you didn't know?" Mrs. Banks looked surprised, then hurriedly continued. "I thought Zan had told you. Maybe she didn't because your friend got killed, so I guess she wanted to wait until after the funeral. I'm so sorry, I thought you knew."

Mrs. Banks might as well have been a dragon. Each word brought an intense heat to Taj's entire body. The roaring in his head prevented him from hearing whatever else she said; he just saw her lips moving. He slightly felt Mrs. Banks' hand on his arm. With a violent shake, he detached himself and rapidly walked to the exit, seeing red.

That bitch lied! The thought broke through his internal drumbeat. Every word, even down to when she was laying in that hospital bed, ran through his mind. If she lied and continued to lie about the pregnancy, was it possible she lied about Lissa too?

When he made it to his car, he just sat there. Lissa's look of hurt and disbelief was forefront on his mind, along with what he said to her. Not wanting to rush judgment again, he decided to find out the truth about everything, before he talked to Zandra or Kalissa.

Ideas of how to find the truth floated around in his head. Cedric's opinion would be valuable, but he had too much going on. Fefe! She was cool with Zan and Lissa, and knew both of them well. When he called her, his call went to voicemail.

"Damn!" He hit his steering wheel.

A car honked at him, waiting for him to back out of the parking space. Taj didn't feel like being closed in his apartment. So, instead of going home, he hit the interstate. As he sped down the near empty highway, heading east, he thought about all the signs he missed: Zandra starting arguments to avoid him, not just him, but his dick. Other little things peppered his memory. The last time he had asked her about her decision to have the baby, she didn't seem as passionate about it. Taj had thought she was seeing things his way.

With a rueful shake of his head, he realized that Zandra had played him. Played him well!

***

Any doubt Kalissa had about Nigel and Fefe dissolved with the look of dismay on Fefe's face.

"Uh-uh—" Nigel started.

"I'm so sorry, Lissa, I wanted to tell you, but y'all hooked up so fast." The words rushed out of Fefe's mouth as she jumped up.

Nigel's head snapped around as he glared at Fefe. "Shid, wasn't nothing to tell, you know that bullshit didn't mean nothing." Standing, he held his hand out to Kalissa and lowered his tone. "Lil' mama, I swear on everything I love, I ain't touched this bitch since I met you."

18

Kalissa looked at his hand but remained motionless. Fefe came between them, hurt shining in her eyes, before she turned on Nigel.

"*Bitch*? Nigga, how the fuck you gonna call me out my name when I told you we needed to tell her. Yo' ass was the one who said not to tell her!"

The look on Nigel's face was hard and mean. He took a menacing step closer to Fefe. "Like I said, there wasn't nothing to tell. You was just something to do and somewhere to lay my head when I needed to."

Kalissa had heard enough. "Stop! Both of you! Just stop it!"

"Lissa, you know I never meant to—"

"Bitch, get the fuck out of my house. I want both of y'all gone!" Kalissa yelled.

"Yeah, hoe, take yo' ass on," Nigel sneered.

"Hold up, homeboy, yo' ass is leaving too. If I don't ever see neither one of y'all asses again, that will be too soon. Thinking y'all gonna play me, huh? Get the fuck out of here!" Kalissa's rage had reached a boiling point.

Nigel sat back down. "I ain't going no damn where."

Fefe stood, looking with tears streaming down her face. Nigel had crossed his arms with a smug look on his face. Everything moved in slow motion for Kalissa. The lies Fefe told her the first time she saw Nigel, him singing and shit to her, probably the same method he used to seduce her friend. Every sweet nothings he had whispered felt false, and what once carried love suddenly felt like bullshit.

Crack! Kalissa slammed her beer bottle across the coffee table, leaving the neck with shards of glass in her hands.

"Y'all wanna leave on foot or on a muthafuckin' stretcher? The choice is yours." Her voice shook with rage.

Fefe began wailing, still apologizing but moving her ass to the door. Kalissa locked eyes with Nigel, every nerve in her body ready for him to make one wrong move, so that she could stab him. Nigel stood and rolled his eyes.

"Lil' mama, you crazy, it ain't that serious." He took a step towards her.

"Oh, my feelings aren't serious? That's what you saying?"

Kalissa saw his hand move too late. She tried to swipe at him with the bottleneck, but he grabbed her wrist. Hard. The glass fell from her hand. Instinctively, her other hand came up and slapped him hard against his ear.

"Damn!" Nigel yelled, pushing her back.

Kalissa stumbled, but caught herself before she fell. Her anger made all common sense leave as she charged him, ready to fight.

"Stop it!" Fefe yelled, as she grabbed Lissa in a bear hug.

"Yo, you crazy!" Nigel yelled.

"Nah, nigga, you ain't seen nothing yet. Let me go, Fefe! Y'all hoes must think I'm something to play wit'!"

"Mane, let me get out of here before I whoop yo' lil' ass," Nigel said before walking out of the door.

"Whoop my ass, nigga. If you feeling froggy, jump!" Kalissa yelled at his back.

No matter how much she squirmed, Fefe still held her. Until she kicked her shins.

"Oww! Lissa, calm yo' ass down!"

"Don't tell me to calm down! Getcha ass out of here, before I give you everythang that was meant for the both of y'all!" Kalissa sputtered in between chest heaves.

"Lissa, whatever you thinking, nothing was done to hurt you. And Nigel is right we haven't been together since he got with you." Fefe's chest shuddered as tears welled in her eyes. "I guess I didn't mean anything to him."

"I hope like hell you ain't thinking I'ma join yo' little pity party. You could have told me way before I met him! I was supposed to have been ya girl. So you knew before now that you was just a piece of ass to him. Especially if you couldn't tell yo' girls about him. Oh wait! You told Zandra's trifling ass, so whateva. All I know is you need to get your ass away from me."

Fefe narrowed her eyes. "Zandra? That's who told you?"

"Fefe, at this point it doesn't matter, I'm not going to ruin y'all's friendship, cuz birds of a feather flock together. I do know one damn thing: when you told her, you knew she was going to tell me. That bitch ain't never wanted to see me happy."

"Lissa—" Fefe reached out with her hand.

"Just get the hell out of here," Lissa spat.

Fefe walked to the door and turned back to Lissa with her hand on the doorknob. "You're not the only one hurting, but I've been hurting in silence for a while now. I was okay hurting because our friendship meant more than anything. I hope you understand that."

When she was met with silence as a response, Fefe quietly walked out.

With slumped shoulders, Kalissa looked around the mess of her living room, which mirrored her life. Hurt, pain and disappointment rushed through her body as she moved slowly, picking up shards of the glass. Unintentional tears ran down her cheeks, stopping at her lips as she tasted the saltiness. Another depiction of her life.

"It doesn't matter. Nobody is meant to stay, everybody always leaves." This had been her mantra ever since her mother had left years before. Instead of making her feel vindicated, as it usually did, she felt barren and completely alone. Instead of just burying a friend, she'd buried two of her closest friends and the love of her life. All in one day.

I've got to put myself in a position where when people leave, it doesn't hurt, she thought as the last shard of glass nicked her finger, drawing blood.

C.D. Blue

Chapter Three

Taj drove while drinking and getting high. He still wanted to vent, but there was nobody else to talk to. Fefe had never called him back. The craziest thing was, the person he wanted to talk to the most was Lissa. Taj shook his head.

Once he slowed down, he realized he was close to the cemetery where his dad was buried. It was dark and the little stretch of road was narrow, but he maneuvered to the area where the grave was. He would never forget that spot.

The night seemed quieter at the cemetery than the rest of the city. As he stumbled through the graveyard, he tried not to step on any graves, but he was too drunk to miss them all. His eyes watered as he approached his dad's final resting place. There were fresh flowers, and the grave had been cleaned off, so he knew his mom had been here recently. Taj sat down heavily next to the headstone.

"Hey, Pops, it's me. I know I haven't been out here to see you like I should and I'm sorry. But it's hard, ya know? I get so wrapped in living, but I haven't forgotten you. There ain't too many days that I don't think about you. You were supposed to be here with me. I can't say for certain that I would have done things different, but maybe I would have if you had guided me. I don't know, man." Taj stopped as his voice cracked.

Although he knew no one else was out there, he still looked around before he continued. "I can't say that you would be proud of me, cuz I know you didn't want me in the streets. But here I am! According to Ma, I'm following in your footsteps."

Taj was nine when his dad was killed. For a long time he thought someone had tried to rob him and then killed him. It wasn't until he was a teenager that his mom told him that he was killed from 'hanging around his good for nothing brother, James. When he asked his uncle, there was so much pain and misery in his face, he just told him: *Never mind.* So, in reality, Taj still didn't know what happened to his Pops.

Sitting there on the hard ground, Taj drank Crown Royal straight out of the bottle, and looked into the darkness for answers. He knew his dad had a job, because he remembered him coming in from work everyday in blue coveralls covered in grease. Many weekends though, his Pops would leave for long periods of time. That's when the fights between his dad and mom would occur. Taj always seemed to be the one to hear them. He remembered hating his Pops, and how guilty he felt for that hatred when he was killed.

"I'm working, Pops, but I'm in the streets too. More in the streets than I should be. I kinda fucked up, man." His voice broke again, but this time he let the tears flow.

"Ma put me out when she found out I was dealing, so I'm not there to be the man I know you wanted me to be. I can't take care of the family like I know you would've wanted me to. I check on them, but Ma—she don't want me to stay around too long. I just don't know what to do, cuz if I stop now, I'll be broke." Taj wiped his nose with the back of his hand.

With his back against the headstone, he nodded off a little bit. Not for long though, because everything he wanted to get off his chest wouldn't let him sleep.

"Then I was mad about that, cuz I ain't living no dangerous life for Ma to treat me like that. But then Cet's— you don't know Cet, anyway, his cousin got killed. Man, I feel like it's my fault! Cuz I lured him and his brother into the game. Damn! I'm just fucked up all over. I mean me and Zo don't even talk no more cuz of this shit!" He sipped some more out of the bottle.

Tears clouded his vision. "Pops, I'm scared." As soon as the words left his mouth, he looked around. "I mean people act like I'm soft and I'm not! I'm yo' son and I want you to know that you didn't raise no punk."

Taj wiped his nose with the back of his hand, and dried his eyes with his shirt. "I've got to show them who I am. Let 'em know that ain't no bitch in me! I don't mean to be cussing and shit, but I'm a man now. I just came here cuz I don't have nobody else to talk to. I fucked around, and put the word of a *hoe*," he spat the last word, "over my best friend. So, I lost her too."

24

The rustling of the leaves in the cemetery made him pause and once again look around. Nothing but silence and ghosts of all the people who found this place as their final resting place. Without even thinking, he ran his hand across his dad's tombstone lovingly before he continued.

"I don't know why I brought my troubles here, cuz Ma told me that people be lying talking about dead folks watching over them. She said the only dead folks watching us are the ones in hell, cuz they waiting on us to join them." Taj laughed as he remembered her saying that. "You know Ma, she keep it real." He sniffled before going on.

"I just wanted to tell you that I'm gonna do what I need to do. I still remember you telling me that my name was all I had. Depending on how it turns out, I might see you sooner than later, but I ain't trying to." Taj looked at the empty spaces next to his Pop's grave.

"I'll be alright. I'm going to make things good between me and everybody. Once my money is up, I'm getting out the game. I'll make you and Ma proud, just watch. I love you, Pops, that's forever." This was the last thing he said before stumbling back to his car.

***

The banging on her door woke Kalissa up. Not wanting to be bothered, she shifted on the sofa where she had fallen asleep. The banging continued. Kalissa sat up, making a face at the nasty taste in her mouth, and looked around. The mess from the night before was swept up, but still remained in a neat pile with the broom propped against the wall near it. She had literally put on every sad song she could think of and cried herself to sleep.

Another bang made her jump.

"All right!" she yelled, going to the door.

It was Nigel! Standing behind the door, she was torn with what to do. Usually, after breaking up with someone, Kalissa would never let them see her mess. Also, usually, they didn't come around the next day either. With her shoulder squared, she opened the door. His lying ass deserved her morning breath.

"What up?" he said as if nothing was wrong.

"What do you want?" Kalissa snapped.

"Come on, now, don't act like that," he tried to charm his way inside.

"Naw, you don't need to think you gonna keep playing wit' me. I said what do you want?"

Nigel shifted from one foot to the other, almost as if he had to pee. "Look, we need to talk. Can you let me in to do that?"

"Humph," was the only answer she gave as she moved back from the door.

"Damn, lil' mama, why you didn't put this shit in trash?" he yelled when he saw the pile of glass.

"Fuck you, nigga," she shot back, as she walked to the bathroom.

Kalissa's eyes grew big when she looked in the mirror. Her breath was the least of her worries! Her hair stood up on her head. Thanks to sweating on the couch, the imprint of the pillow ridges was on the right side of her face. She looked a mess!

Then on top of looking a mess, she felt sweaty and musty. A shower was needed but she did not want Nigel getting too comfortable. Instead, she just wiped up under her arms, brushed her teeth and washed her face. Along with brushing her hair back. This was the best that he would get from her.

Nigel was putting the broom back in the kitchen when she stomped out the bathroom, ready to fight.

"Why are you here again?" Kalissa stood with her arms crossed.

"You trippin' I swear, you know Fefe don't mean shit to me. Fuck! I met you at her spot. If me and her were heavy like that, do you think I would have been all up on you like that?"

Nigel's brown eyes were alluring with his passion. Kalissa knew Fefe, though. It might not have been anything to him, but her friend would do anything to have a man. Even stay in the shadows.

"Nah, it ain't even about all that! Both of you lied to me. Straight up lied, in-my-face lies. How you think I feel knowing she knows what it's like to be wit' you? Then both of you smiling in my face like we having some damn family reunion. Nah, I don't play them type of games."

"Man, you making a big deal out of nothing." Nigel walked over to the couch and sat down.

"Nothing? Then of all things, that bitch Zandra knew. So, this whole time I'm thinking I'm happy, she was behind my back laughing at me. That shit is foul. I don't care how you spin it."

Kalissa had begun pacing. "Matter of fact, you can get out. I don't want to hear it or see you."

Nigel's brown eyes turned serious. "I'm not going anywhere. Fefe is your homegirl. As far as I knew, she told you about us."

"Don't do that. You know damn well if I knew about y'all, one, I wouldn't have fooled wit' you and two, I would have asked you about it. Just take your sorry excuses somewhere else." Lissa rolled her eyes.

"Naw, I ain't going. I love you and I'm gonna be here for my baby."

Kalissa's head snapped around. "What baby?"

"The one you're pregnant with, that baby. My son," Nigel said smugly with a grin.

"You crazy! I ain't having yo' baby!" Kalissa shot back.

"What you gonna do, then? You ain't having no abortion, cuz I don't believe in that."

Fear raced through her body as she tried to remember her last period. With all the fun of being in love, then Desi getting killed, she really hadn't paid attention. With Jamila she hadn't gotten sick, only with that devil's baby.

Nigel laughed. "You might not have noticed but I did. Plus, I know what pregnant pussy feels like."

"Nah, you talking crazy. I'm not pregnant and you still need to go." Kalissa was shaking her head and walking to the door.

Nigel grabbed her and picked her up from behind, ignoring her kicks and yells.

"Come here, woman, I'm tired of you trying be a little bad ass," he said, as he dropped her on the bed.

Still kicking and wriggling around, Kalissa gasped when she felt the coolness hit her bottom.

"Aw, hell naw!" she yelped, wiggling around some more.

Nigel grabbed both of her feet with one hand and when she felt his hot tongue against her slit, all fight left her. The yells turned to moans, and the next thing she knew: she felt relief once he slid inside of her.

"Damn, this pussy is hot and wet," Nigel moaned.

Just like that they were back together.

Chapter Four

As hard as his head was banging, Taj still snatched the covers off and stomped to the bathroom. After a piss that never seemed to end, he turned the shower on while he brushed his teeth. Once he cleaned up, he dressed carefully, not as neat as usual, but still holding onto his swag.

Taj grimaced before putting his phone in his pocket. Fifteen messages and twenty missed calls from Zan.

"I guess that bitch head feeling better now," he muttered.

Racing through the city with his windows down and music blaring, scenes passed through his mind like a movie. Desi in that damn casket, he and Duke's mom breaking down, and Zandra lying at the bottom of his stairs.

"Yo' mane, I'm pulling up," he said.

Cet was sitting on the porch when he pulled into the driveway. When Taj got closer, he saw that Cet looked worse than him.

"You hanging in there?" Taj said, looking towards inside of the house.

"Mane, I just keep wishing this shit is some kind of dream and I'm going to wake up," Cet said. "I mean I pulled him into this shit. Ain't nobody said nothing but I see the way my whole family been looking at me since this happened. Duke got out of here so quick last night. Shid."

"I feel the same way. I keep seeing his face, mane. That's why we need to hit back at them 'Skegee niggas," Taj spat.

"For real? You down for that, cuz? Fuck yeah, I'm ready. We can do this shit today." A little light sparked in Cet's eyes.

"I'ma call Rod first and then we need to round up some of the crew. Anybody ain't down for it, got to go."

"That's on everythang I love. I'm ready for this shit," Cet said while he jumped up.

Taj cocked his head to the right. "Yo Cet, you remember that lil' red boy that was stealing from me that time? You don't think he would've tried something? He had hella attitude and I know he was mad at me."

"Nah, I know for sure it wasn't him. Somebody killed him before this shit happened." Cet shook his head.

"Damn! Fa real? He must have stole from the wrong one. I hate that shit though; he was just a kid. Was he still in the game?" Taj asked, trying to ignore the hurt look that crossed Cet's face. He knew he was thinking about Desi.

"Yeah, I think Zo had pulled him into Rollo's crew." Cet picked some imaginary lint off his pants.

"I didn't know that. Well, did Rollo go after whoever did it?"

"Nah, man. Rollo ain't like that. He don't operate off loyalty, it's straight fear in his camp. Them niggas know he crazy and if they end up dead, Rollo just keep rolling." Cet laughed at his own joke.

Taj looked puzzled. "Shidd, them niggas got to fear the streets and their leader? That's fucked up."

"Mane, them niggas getting paid. Rollo might not give a shit about them, but he keep their pockets lined. Fasho."

Taj's phone had been vibrating in his pocket the entire time he was talking to Cet. Figuring it was Zandra, he needed to be in his car to give that hoe the business. "I'll holla at you in a minute. I'll get at Rod, then let you know something."

Before he started his car, he looked at his phone and saw it was Fefe running him down. Before he could call her back, his phone rang in his hand.

"Taj! I missed yo' call last night. What's going on with Zan? Are you at the hospital?" Fefe screeched in his ear.

"Hold up! She's fine and I'm not at the hospital cuz I'm through with her lying ass!" Taj said evenly.

"What? What the hell is going on, Taj? How you gonna leave her in a time like this?"

Taj frowned at his phone. Fefe sounded as if she was crying. Although he knew her and Zandra were friends, he didn't think they were that close.

"Where you at?"

"Home. I was about to go to the hospital, but I don't know," she sniffed loudly into the phone.

"Hang tight, I'll be right there," he said before hanging up.

Taj shot Rod a text. He looked towards the house, but Cet had gone inside, so Taj made his way to Fefe's. It didn't take more than twenty minutes to get anywhere in the city and since Fefe lived on the same side that he was on, he pulled up in seven minutes.

When she answered the door, Taj took a step back. Fefe looked a wreck! Usually, she was always put together, but she had on her pajamas, her hair was all over her head and it looked as if she hadn't washed her face.

"Damn, you must have gotten fucked up last night!" he joked.

With a roll of her eyes and neck, she pushed her lips out. "Don't act like you haven't talked to Lissa. I know she told you what happened."

"Nah, I haven't. What happened?" Taj sat down across from her in the chair.

Adjusting the bottom of her pajama shirt, Fefe mumbled, "She found out that me and Nigel used to mess around."

"Say what?"

"Yeah. I would've told her if I had thought they were going to get serious, but you know how Lissa is. She'll talk to someone for a little while then stop. I thought it would be same for her and Nigel."

"So, Nigel told Lissa?" Taj overlooked that Fefe had plenty of time to tell her girl about the guy she was fucking.

"Hell nah, that lying ass nigga was still trying to deny it when she confronted us. Fuck boy!" she spat. "I think Zandra told her. I don't know, she never said. That bitch just threw us out." Fefe looked hurt and angry at the same time.

"You told Zandra but didn't tell Lissa? That's kinda of fucked up, Fefe. You know how they are." Taj shook his head.

Pushing up to the end of the sofa, Fefe's eyes blazed in anger. "You know I ain't that stupid. Zandra found out way before Nigel and Lissa got together. I didn't think she would tell because, hell, they never talk. I had never told Lissa cuz it wasn't serious, and you know how she gets sometimes. One day she's cool wit' jus' having fun and the next she's giving a speech 'bout not letting men eat their cake and have it too. I didn't want to hear that shit, I just wanted to have fun in peace."

"And you knew Zan would be down for that bullshit. Figures."

"Nah, it wasn't like that. Like I said, Zan found out by accident. Anyway, speaking of Zandra, why aren't you at the hospital?" Fefe stood up and walked towards the kitchen. She stopped at his chair, waiting for an answer.

"Because Zan is a lying hoe! She lied about still being pregnant so I know she lied about Lissa pushing her down the stairs." Taj felt the anger from last night return.

"Pregnant? Zan told you she was pregnant? Humph, that doesn't sound right. I could have told you that was probably a lie." Fefe laughed, continuing to the kitchen.

Taj followed her. "How would you know?"

"Tee, don't you remember when Zan used to miss school all the time?"

Thinking back, he nodded and Fefe continued.

"She used to have real bad periods and after her mom took her to the doctor, they told her she had something called epidemi, or something. Anyway, she told me and Lissa that the doctor told her that she would probably never be able to have children or never carry them full term. That damn girl is a trip!"

A beer was shoved in his hand as she spoke. Taj twisted the top off and took a long pull.

Taj thought about the times Zan would be laid up in the bed, complaining about her cycle. He thought she just wanted some attention or was making excuses as to why she couldn't keep a job. "Nah, she was pregnant, I guess, but her mom said she had a miscarriage. Lissa knew about it too, huh? I mean, Zan's condition?"

"Yeah, but you know how she is. Once she's done with you, it's like you don't exist for her anymore, so she may have forgotten. And you say Zan said Lissa pushed her down the stairs? She needs to stop with that bullshit." Fefe took a sip of beer. "Now if she had said Lissa beat her ass down the stairs, I would believe it. But something sneaky like pushing her? I doubt that, very seriously."

Everything Fefe said was true, and made Taj feel like a bigger fool. That's probably why Lissa had that look on her face, not because she had done it. She might have remembered that Zandra couldn't be pregnant.

"Damn and I accused her of killing my baby. I got to make things right with her. That's my homegirl and I fucked up."

"Zan told you she lost the baby from falling down the steps? Lawd, that girl knows she a drama queen." Fefe was still standing in front of her sofa, looking out the window. With a shake of her head, she blew out a deep breath.

When Fefe plopped down on the sofa, Taj almost heard the pillows yell for help. "She'll probably forgive you way before she forgives me. You were just caught up in Zandra's mess, she thinks I betrayed her. I promise you, Tee, I wasn't trying to. I just didn't know how to tell her. One night they are playing around and the next thing you know, they were a couple. I just didn't want to hurt her."

Taj believed Fefe, but he also knew it was fucked up. Lissa would forgive, but she never forgot when somebody hurt her. He thought about how close Lissa and Zan used to be. However, Zandra had hurt her. Lissa had to be nursing a deep wound. Fefe was right, it would probably be a long time if ever when she was forgiven.

His phone dinged with a text. Taking it out of his pocket, he saw that Rod had hit him back.

"Look, I gotta run. Just give her a few days. She'll think about it and change her mind." Taj walked towards the door.

"Yeah, right. I might go see Zandra later. You want me to tell her anything?" Fefe came up behind him.

Taj paused in the doorway. "Yeah, tell her to stop calling me."

C.D. Blue

Chapter Five

"What you thinking about, pretty lady?" Nigel's voice broke her concentration.

"Nothing. Well, actually, I was thinking that if I am pregnant, I don't think I'm ready for another baby," Kalissa said softly.

"You might as well get ready, cuz I don't believe in abortion. You ain't killing my baby," Nigel said, forcibly moving his arm from up under her.

Even after a day spent sexing, eating and talking, then a night with more of the same, Kalissa still hadn't gotten over the hurt about him and Fefe. To think that she might be pregnant made her feel ten times worse. No matter how much she tried to say they were just friends with benefits, she had seen the hurt in Fefe's eyes when Nigel denied her. Just as she had seen her friend's hurt, she was sure that Fefe had seen how much it hurt her.

"Boy, hush. Don't nobody want to hear all that this early. Go back to sleep." Lissa turned her back to him.

"See, that's your problem right there, you always trying to tell me what to do. You don't run me, woman! Come here," Nigel growled, pulling her closer to him.

"Oh no, get that loaded weapon off my back." She giggled, feeling his dick poke her.

"I might need to shoot it off in you, I can't be walking around with a loaded weapon," Nigel whispered, licking the middle of her back.

The heat of his tongue made her stomach flip, but she was sore as hell from the last twenty-four hours.

"Nope, not this morning. My pussy can't get wet even if I wanted it to. Anyway, I need to go pick up Jamila."

Kalissa got up and looked back at him, almost feeling bad at the disappointment in his face. All sympathy stopped when she had to hop to the bathroom because her legs were so sore.

"You want to ride with me?"

"To pick up Jamila from your dad's?"

"Nah, nigga, to the circus. Yes, from my dad's," Kalissa joked.

"You know you got a smart-ass mouth. Yeah, I guess it's time to meet the family, since you having my baby," Nigel shot back.

He started singing "Forever My Lady" by Jodeci. It sounded good, but Kalissa just gave him a look, until he grabbed her waist and began kissing her face.

"You not singing me back to the bed. Come on, let's get ready so that we can get back before night," Lissa laughed, pushing him away.

Once they were dressed, they got on the road. Kalissa listened to the old-school music, while Nigel sang and danced the whole trip. Each time certain songs came on, he glanced at her, asking if she knew what year it came out. Other than that, they didn't talk much. Which was a good thing because all she wanted to ask him about was his relationship with Fefe. She couldn't let it go.

As they drove down the winding road that led to her dad's, she looked at the houses that belonged to her uncles as they passed. With most of their kids grown, the homes looked lonely and empty. Two lions stood on columns at the entrance of the drive. Nigel stopped and looked at her after he peeped at the huge house behind the fence.

"This is where your dad lives?" Nigel's mouth gaped in wonder.

"Yep," was all she said, as she leaned over him to enter the code.

"You living in the ghetto when you could live here?"

"Umm-hmm, here is out in the country where there is absolutely nothing. Plus, my dad has too many rules," Lissa answered smoothly.

"Shid, can't be that bad. You crazy, lil' mama." Nigel shook his head as he drove down the driveway towards the house.

Jamila jumped on them as soon as they walked in the house.

"Mommy!" She ran and tackled Kalissa.

"Hey, baby, did you have a good time?" Kalissa picked her up and rained kisses all over her face.

"Yes. Nigel!" Her little voice screeched when she noticed him.

Kalissa's dad stood back and watched the family reunion and after she made the introductions, her grandmother made her appearance. Grandma Bina was a force to be reckoned with. Standing under five feet, she ran her family as if she was six feet tall.

"Well, who do we have here?" Grandma Bina said in her gravelly voice.

Once more introducing Nigel again, Kalissa gave her grandmother a hug and sat down on the leather sectional. Jamila sat right beside her.

"Come on outside, let me see what you're driving," her dad told Nigel.

Nigel followed him outside and when Kalissa rose to follow, her grandmother stopped her.

"Let the men talk amongst themselves."

There was nothing left to do but sit down. Her grandmother told her about everything that Jamila had done, while Kalissa stole peeks toward the outside.

"Mommy, look," Jamila burst out, throwing her hands in Lissa's face.

Her fingernails were painted light pink, and then she took her shoes off to show off her matching toes.

"Oh, my! You like that?" Kalissa purred.

Jamila nodded. She was such a girlie girl, and Lissa had no idea where that came from. Resentment eased into her bones as she thought of all the things she could have known to do as a woman, if her mom had bothered to stay and raise her. Growing up, she had been a tomboy, but once she noticed that she liked boys a lot, there was so much that having a mother would have helped with. Not to mention the domestic things, such as cooking.

"Why are you frowning over there?" her grandmother asked.

"No reason, I was just thinking about how I never liked polishing my nails and stuff like that," Kalissa answered smoothly.

It wouldn't help to tell her grandmother what she was thinking because her dad's side of the family felt some type of way towards her mother anyway.

The rest of the trip was uneventful. Nigel and her dad came back in. They ate a huge meal and got ready to depart.

"Little Jamila shole likes your boyfriend and he's seems good with her. I know you will keep your baby safe, but *you* be careful." Grandma whispered in her ear before they left.

Surprised by the comment, Kalissa pushed away and looked at her grandmother. "I will be, or at least try."

"Do you love him?" her grandmother persisted.

Lissa looked towards the car where Nigel was strapping Jamila into her car seat.

"Yes, I do, I truly love him," she smiled.

"Then love him freely, okay?"

Her grandmother hugged her tightly while her dad gave her a hug, along with instructions about her car.

The ride was mostly silent until Nigel broke it suddenly. "That's the house yo' mom left y'all in?"

With a sigh and chuckle, she chose her words carefully. "Nope. We lived in Ridgecrest when my mom left. My dad didn't move there until I left home, after he won that lawsuit. You know he's originally from the country, so I guess he wanted to go back to his roots. But even before then my mom didn't have to work unless she wanted to."

"Damn, I bet she regret that shit now, yo' dad is living large," Nigel chuckled.

They made it back to Montgomery before it got dark, and Nigel made a detour to the CVS.

"Stay right here, I'll be right back," he said quickly.

Kalissa looked back at Jamila sleeping peacefully in her car seat. The notification bell on her phone went off, and she rummaged through her purse, looking for it. When she was with Nigel, she paid her phone no attention whatsoever.

Her lips touched her nose as she saw she had a text from Taj and a number she didn't recognize. Skipping over Taj's message, just because she was not ready to deal with him, she looked at the other one. It was from Zandra!

I guess you finally got what you wanted bitch!

Not knowing what she was talking about, it still pissed her off that this hoe had the audacity to even think to text her. With a quick tap, she set her fingertips to respond, but curiosity got the best of her. She peeped at Taj's text.

Call me when you get a chance. We need to talk.

Lissa closed her text messages. "Not today, I will not let them mess up my day," she said to no one.

"Who you talking to?" Nigel said, as he hopped in the driver's seat.

"Nobody, I was talking to myself."

Nigel glanced suspiciously at her phone in her lap. He didn't say anything, but his jaw started working.

"Can we just go home?" Kalissa asked.

"Umm-hmm, that's where we going," Nigel mumbled.

Kalissa looked out of the window the entire ride, just wishing there could be one full day without some shit!

C.D. Blue

Chapter Six

"Girl, I thought you were still in the hospital. I'm glad you're okay, but when you hear somebody done fell down the stairs, you think they gonna be out for a while." Fefe glanced over at Zandra.

Fefe had called Zandra, hoping to make a short visit at the hospital, just to say she checked on her. Much to her surprise, Zan was at home and other than the bruises on her face and the two casts, she looked much better than Fefe expected

"I was pushed. You know what it's like when someone gets pushed down the stairs," Zandra scrunched her face up.

Fefe smacked her lips and rolled her eyes. "You might try that with Taj, but I know better. Lissa did not push you down no stairs!"

Zandra pushed herself up on her pillows with her good arm, and sniffed loudly. "Everybody thinks she's so perfect. Taj won't even return my calls because he thinks I'm lying about what she did!"

Fefe's wig started feeling tight the more Zandra talked. Patting the sides of her short do down, she tried to choose her words carefully.

"Is that really what happened?"

Zandra's nostrils flared. "Yeah. What you mean is that what really happened? You know Taj has always chosen that bitch over me."

"Aht, aht! I'm talking about her pushing you down! Stop lying, Zan! I already know that you lied about still being pregnant. You need to cut this bullshit out!" Fefe raised her voice, and stood up from the side of the bed where she'd been sitting.

With narrowed eyes, Zandra sat up. "I felt her hands, so yeah, she pushed me. How did you know about—? What did you tell him, Fefe?"

"Nah, the question is: why did you tell Lissa about me and Nigel? You was wrong for that!" Fefe's chest rose and fell heavily.

"Chile, that's what you mad about? It slipped out cuz she was acting so high and mighty. I just told her that she was just like me." Zandra said those words dismissively while lying back on her pillows.

"That's some foul shit! You fucked Terry while they were together. Me and Nigel was just fooling around and had ended that shit before they even met. I can't trust yo' ass for nothing! I hate that you ever found out about me and him."

"Whatever, the fact still remains that she pushed me down the stairs. I was going to tell Taj that I had lost the baby, but he was being so sweet then his friend died, so I hadn't gotten around to it. Who knew my momma would spill the beans wit' her big mouth! Whether I hadn't told him that part, doesn't mean I lied about that damn Lissa. That's the part you and Taj still seem to forget." Zandra twisted her lips.

"Well, I don't believe she did it cuz I know her, and Taj doesn't believe it because you lied about still being pregnant. When you start all that lying, that makes everything you say suspect."

"I know what I felt. If she wasn't assisting my fall, why did she have her hands on me? And we walked out right after I told her yo' lil' secret. She was mad as hell." Zandra fell back on her pillows.

The bed sunk in as Fefe sat back down on the edge. She glanced towards Zandra's bedroom door nervously. "I just can't see Lissa doing nothing like that, for real."

"You're thinking about the Kalissa, the one who likes you. I'm talking about Lissa, once you're on her shit list. Now that you're on that list, you betta watch yo' back." Zandra finished with a big sigh and closed her eyes.

"I'm not worried about that. There's no reason for her to stay mad at me, I don't want Nigel," Fefe said, quietly sitting back down on the edge of the bed.

Zandra narrowed her eyes and smirked. "Shit! You think I wanted Terry? That bitch kept talking about his big dick and how good he smashed her, I wanted to see for myself. And that's not what you said when you told me about Nigel. He was all that and then some."

In a voice laced with confidence, Fefe said: "You know what? Anyway, that was before Lissa got involved and I was done playing games wit' that nigga before they got together. I'll give her a little while to cool off, then we'll be back cool."

Zandra was twisting two strands of her blanket together with her good arm. She gave her friend a sly look.

"You might as well join my club. You know Lissa may forgive you, but she ain't gonna never forget. That girl don't give a shit for real about nobody."

A heavy sigh escaped Fefe's mouth. "Zan, you know that isn't true. Yes, Lissa can be hard, but we both know her way back. I'm still not sure if I believe you. I just can't see her doing that. There has to be some good explanation. You know she's good people."

Zandra rolled her eyes. "That's how she gets away wit' most of the shit she does. Can't nobody see her doing shit. I don't care what you believe, I know what that hoe did to me!"

"That's not true. I know there are some things she's done, but one thing about it, if she meant it, she'll tell it. If you had just apologized when she found out instead of lying, y'all would still be friends. That's my plan, although I already apologized once, but there was too much going on. Taj told me to give her a few days." Fefe regretted the words as soon as they came out of her mouth.

Zandra slapped her good hand on her pillow. "Oh, so you can talk to him about her, but not take up for me? Ain't that some shit!"

All Fefe heard was jealousy. Her words pissed her off, but Fefe also felt sorry for her. "Damn, bitch! I was talking to him about my problems. It's up to you to make up for yo' mistakes. What? You want him to be mad at me too?" Fefe immediately felt guilty for her outburst. She tried to make up for it. "Don't worry, y'all will get back together."

"Humph. I sure hope so. Whether we get back together or not, Lissa gonna find out she ain't the only one who don't forget shit.

That bitch tried to kill me and I won't ever forget that. Her day is coming. I promise you that and I don't care how long it takes either."

Fefe's shoulder slumped at her friend's words. "Girl, don't say shit like that! We all need to get past this bullshit and just put it behind us. Don't you remember how much fun we use to have? If you talking like that, things ain't gonna never be right."

Zandra's face changed from anger back to regular in an instant.

"Okay, you'll see. When that hoe show you and Tee her true colors, I'm here to tell ya, I'ma say I told you so!"

Fefe didn't respond, she just looked sad. Zandra switched gears and removed the hate out of her tone.

"Since Tee ain't answering my calls, I guess I'm officially back on the market. As soon as I get this shit off me, I'ma hit the streets! But this time I'ma find me a real baller."

***

As soon as dusk fell, Cet and Taj met at Rod's place. Taj expected to see Nigel, but he was nowhere to be found. Rod had gathered a carload of his crew, and four of Taj's runners were coming along too. They were the four with the biggest mouths. Taj needed the word to get back to everybody that he did not play about any of his men.

When he told them the plan, he knew he had made the right choice by the way their faces lit up. No more Mr. Nice Guy.

"I think we should storm their trap from the back and leave them all wet up," Cet said to Rod.

"Nah, mane. I rode by there a couple of times. It's a two story house. If we come from the back, somebody upstairs can easily hit us. We gonna send a message. If somebody come out trying to be Rambo, we dead 'em. If somebody get hit on the inside, that's just how it happens. You don't want yo' boys thinking you set them up for a suicide mission," Rod said before letting a wad of spit hit the pavement.

"I feel ya. That makes sense. But why we just sending a message?" Cet wasn't ashamed about learning the ropes. Rod knew that he had never done anything like this before.

Rod rubbed his chin. "I'ma jus' keep it real. Y'all ain't one hunnid that these niggas did that shit. I ain't heard nothing in the streets and to be honest, them 'Skegee niggas too pussy, fa real. I don't wanna murk nobody then find out they didn't do it. Even if it's years from now. I already got enough shit on me." Rod gave a rare smile, showing off his gold grill.

Cet nodded, soaking in the knowledge.

"You right, my nigga," Taj gave Rod a fist bump.

"After we send the message, then if they did anything, niggas will talk. Somebody gonna tell, then to explain why they'll cop that shit. Even if it's just for street cred. If we hear that, then we go in fa' real! And that's on everythang! We'll load up in a lil' while. We can catch them niggas before they hit the blocks." Rod turned and started walking towards the house.

"Aye, mane, we going to get something to eat." Taj yelled at his back. Rod raised his arm in response.

"You wanna eat now?" Cet scrunched up his face.

"Mane, we ain't never did this shit before. This might be our last damn meal."

Realization hit Cet's face before he followed Taj to his car.

Once they pulled off from the house, he and Cet started talking about what they just learned.

Taj began, "That shit made a lot of sense. Jus' between you and me, I ain't sure if I'm ready to kill nobody anyway."

"Me either. But if I find out who murked Desi, I'll be on go, then. I don't want to kill nobody that didn't do shit, though. But, them niggas that drew on us, they ass done some shit, I bet!" Cet was looking out the window. "I understand what Rod was saying. And he's right, somebody will start running they mouth."

"Yep. And if they didn't do it, they'll know they can't be pulling out they stick on us and get away with it." Taj was warming up to the mission the more he talked about it.

"Who the fuck else could it be? These was the only niggas that pulled their sticks out," Cet shot back through gritted teeth.

"Nigga, they may have been the only ones who threatened y'all wit that heat, but they wasn't the only niggas that y'all rubbed the wrong damn way. And you know these niggas in the Gump are grimy and two-faced."

That statement caught Cet's attention because he rubbed his chin as he looked out the window.

"You know what? There was these niggas at Applebee's one day that we got into with."

"Applebee's?" Lissa's job?" Taj slammed on brakes to avoid rear-ending the car in front of him.

"Yeah, Lissa was there. I dunno who they was, but they was talking mad shit until we shut it down. I wonder if she knows them." Cet pulled his phone out, but Taj stopped him.

"Nah, man, don't call her right now. She probably won't answer anyway," Taj said as he glided into the Burger King parking lot.

"Why not?"

When Taj didn't answer immediately, Cet looked around. "Burger King, nigga? This might be possibly be our last damn meal? You tripping," Cedric laughed.

Taj laughed with him, but that did not throw Cet off track.

"You still didn't answer my question. Why can't I call Lissa? What you did?" Cet looked at Taj.

"We kinda had it out . . ." Taj began before giving Cet the short version of the story.

Cet laughed into his fist. "Wait, you mean to tell me you accused Lissa of killing a baby that Zan had lost? Mane, stop lying! I know you didn't do no shit like that! What the fuck Lissa going to throw Zan big ass down the stairs for anyway?"

"Mane, that shit ain't funny. I don't know. They was in my place by themselves for a while and you know how them two are. Next thing I know, Zan's ass was coming down the stairs head-first. Then, once I found out her ass had lied, I wanted to punch that hoe in the mouth." Taj cut his eyes at Cet, who was laughing hysterically.

"Mane, I wish I could've seen that shit! If Lissa did push her, remind me not to make her mad, shit!" Some more laughter followed.

"Mane, that shit ain't funny," Taj said, although he chuckled a little too.

They ordered and as soon as Taj paid for the order, Rod texted him saying they were ready to ride.

"Let's just get this shit over," Taj said as they headed back to Rod's.

The ride to Tuskegee was tense. One of Rod's men—Jojo— was in the backseat; since they didn't know him, Taj and Cet stayed quiet. They were three cars deep and the closer they got, the more Taj questioned his decision. His stomach knotted with his indecision.

"Yo man, when we get off the exit, turn that shit down," Jojo barked from the backseat.

Jojo was short with more chest than neck, but obviously someone had told him he was the shit because that was how he acted.

"Nigga, we know that! We ain't stupid," Cet snapped in response.

Jojo mumbled something under his breath. He acted as if riding with them was beneath him or some type of burden. Whatever he was thinking, he had a bad attitude about it.

"Turn up there!" Cet pointed to the next block excitedly.

The only thing Tuskegee had going for them was the college. The rest of the city was nothing special, especially the area they were in. Shack houses with cars in the yard, most of them on bricks. No lights, just pure country.

"It's the second one to the corner," Cet barked.

Jojo was on his phone relaying the info to Rod. "Ride past it first, then come back around," he directed.

Cet cut his eyes to the back while getting his choppa ready. Taj did what he was told and at the second pass by right before they got to the house, Jojo yelled out.

"Now! Fire that bitch up."

Blatt, blatt, blatt, blatt, bop, bop! was all Taj heard, along with glass breaking as half of Cet's body hung out the window.

"Go, nigga, go!" Jojo yelled.

Taj floored it, ignoring Cet's yell as he almost fell out of the car. He made it around the corner and screeched through the neighborhood until he saw the main road. It wasn't until they were back on the interstate that he noticed how much he was sweating. When he glanced in his rearview mirror, he caught Jojo's eyes and his smirk.

Chapter Seven

It was getting dark, and Taj felt like a stalker. He was sitting in his car outside of Kalissa's job, waiting for her to come out. The entire week he had sent her texts that went unanswered. That had changed this morning. She responded with a dry 'hey' to his good morning. It was a start, and it gave him enough nerve to come by her job.

Ten minutes later, he saw her peep out of the side door. Kalissa squinted, and he knew she had seen him when a look of annoyance crossed her face. Taj chuckled, but there was no escape plan for her since he parked right beside her.

Kalissa's stride was purposeful and hard as she walked out to her car, still not looking his way.

Taj stepped out of his car. "Lissa, come on now. How long you plan on ignoring me?"

Lissa stopped outside of her car with the door open. Without turning around, she answered, "Forever."

By this time, he had made it to her car. Standing on the other side of her door, he looked at her. "Lissa, I'm sorry. Mane, we better than this. I just want to talk to you."

The sound of her keys hitting against each other was all he heard. Kalissa looked down, still refusing to look at him. When she finally spoke, he heard the hurt in her voice.

"Yeah, I thought we were too, but you showed me we weren't. So, there isn't much to talk about it."

"I was wrong, okay? How can I apologize if you won't let me explain?" Taj yelled in frustration.

Lissa looked towards the restaurant door and at the evening crowd coming in. This time she gave a huge eyeroll.

"Okay, but not here. Meet me at my place. Come to think of it, give me a couple of hours to get Jamila in the bed."

"A'ight, you going to be there?" Taj held the car door open as she got in.

"Mane, don't play me. Why would I tell you to come if I'm not going to be there?" Lissa tried to jerk the door from him.

"Aye, one more thing. What about Nigel? I mean, will he be cool with it? I don't want to step on his toes," Taj said diplomatically.

A sigh that sounded as if it came from her toes escaped from Lissa. "Nigel is well. He'll be alright with it. He's not there tonight anyway. And the only toes you need to worry about are yours. Cuz if you don't move I'm going to run over them."

"All right then, I'll see you in a few," he smiled, but did not get one in return.

By the time he made it over, he had actually given her almost three hours. He had checked on some business, got something to eat, then he stopped and got her favorite beer.

The first thing he noticed when she opened the door was how tired she looked. Taj hoped that Nigel hadn't been fucking around.

"What up? Look what I brought," Taj held up the beer, hoping to get something that resembled a smile. Nothing. It hurt him to see her look at him like that. In all the years they had known each other, he had seen that look before; it just had never been directed at him.

"I'll put it in the fridge. I'm not drinking tonight, I've got to go in tomorrow morning," Lissa said, taking the six-pack from him.

The cold reception gave him a bad case of nerves. He didn't know what to do, so he just stood there.

"Why you still at the door? You gonna sit down or nah?" Kalissa came out of kitchen, talking.

"I wasn't sure if I could, fa real," Taj answered honestly.

"Boy, sit down."

Kalissa's furniture was shaped like a horseshoe, so he sat in the chair, directly across from the television, which was turned off. Kalissa sat on the sofa and pulled her legs under her, then looked at him expectantly.

"Look, Lissa, I'm not going to say I'm sorry again. I should have known that you didn't have nothing to do with Zandra falling. I was just upset and knowing how much y'all hate each other, I just drew the wrong conclusion."

Rubbing her knees she looked at him with her eyebrows raised. "You drew the wrong conclusion? Oh, cuz I thought you said that hoe told you I pushed her. Which one is it? And if you drew the wrong conclusion one time, what made you come to this new conclusion?"

"Well, see—" Taj started.

"Un-uh. Let me address everythang you said, cuz we are having a conversation. I don't hate Zandra, that bitch don't mean shit to me. You always asked why we stopped talking, right?" She stopped as if thinking about something. "Naw, never mind, anyway, carry on with whatever you were about to say." One leg had come off the couch, but Lissa remained seated.

Taj took a deep breath and tried another approach. "Zan did tell me that, and I never thought she would go far enough to tell that kind of lie. But when I went back up, her mom told me that she had lost the baby a few weeks prior." He hung his head. "I knew I had been made a fool of about everything. I fucked up."

When he looked up, he expected to see a mean mug, but instead she looked confused.

"I know you lying! That bitch lost the baby before she fell?" She paused for his response. Taj only nodded.

Lissa cocked her head, seemingly processing everything. She held up her hand. "So, her momma told you that she had a miscarriage?"

Taj once again nodded. Lissa narrowed her eyes. "Sooo, if her momma hadn't told you that she had a miscarriage, you would be still be thinking I had pushed her? You really think that about me? I mean we've only known each other forever. I've had plenty of people fuck over me and none of them got pushed. I guess that's why I'm a bit confused."

Every word came out enunciated and it seemed as if she emphasized each syllable.

Taj looked at her sheepishly. "You shole right and I'm so sorry." He splayed his hands. "I know had I been thinking straight, I wouldn't have come at you like that. I think that even if Mrs. Banks hadn't told me eventually, I would have come to my senses.

51

I just hope you can forgive me. Fa real." Taj looked at Kalissa, waiting for her response.

Kalissa just sat there, seemingly lost in her thoughts, nodding. "I mean, as long as you and I have known each other, you shoulda known that I wouldn't do no shit like that."

Taj noticed that she was not going to let it go easily. He tried another tactic. "Lissa, yes, I know you betta than that. That's why I'm here begging for yo' forgiveness. I was wrong. My head was all screwed up. Desi getting killed, thinking about what I needed to do to straighten that out, I was in a fucked up place."

Still not looking at him, Lissa began to speak. Someone who didn't know her would think she was talking to herself. Taj knew better.

"Forgiveness is a funny thing. My heart is always ready to forgive or can be directed to do it easily." She thumped the side of her head. "But my mind. It's a different story. This mug works on its own. I don't think I have any control. You came at me like it was a fact, didn't give me a chance to explain, wouldn't listen to me, nothing. I can forgive you for all of that, but is it going to heal the hurt in my heart? That's what I don't know."

Kalissa's words hurt him. He swallowed the lump in his throat before he responded. "I'ma do whatever it takes to make that happen. I never wanted to hurt you and as fucked up as I was, there's no excuse."

A deep sigh escaped from Lissa. "You don't have to do anything. Tee, we never gave in to our chemistry because we both knew our friendship was too valuable. You ain't just my friend, you're my brother. I mean, if we gonna hurt each other we might as well have fucked and been a couple!"

Taj laughed, but her next words stopped his laughter.

"I've found with women, they gonna let men and other women come between friendships. They jealous if they think your man treat you better than theirs. They jealous if you have a man and they don't. They jealous if they think you closer than another female. All kinds of shit! You and me, we didn't have that problem. Wasn't nothing supposed to come between us. We were forever solid."

"You right, Lissa. I fucked up and I can't say it no other way. Let me show you rather than tell you. I can't show Desi that I fucked up putting him on, and I'll forever live with that, but I need you to give me a chance to prove it to you," Taj pleaded.

Lissa squinted and smiled. "Oh, I see why the women love you. You're good. You don't have anything to prove about nothing. Even about Desi. That was not your fault. We all have to live with the choices we make."

"No matter what you say, I still feel like I led Desi to his death. He just wanted to make a lil' cash, not get killed. And I know Cet feels the same way, probably worse. I don't know. It's just all fucked up."

"It's not your fault, Tee. They came to you and we all young, but we ain't kids no more. Even if they haven't been nowhere, they have seen this shit on T.V. I hate it happened too, but you can't blame yourself. The only person to blame is the nigga who did it. And I'm guessing y'all still don't know who that is," Kalissa said slowly.

"Nah, and that shit right there is driving Cet crazy. That nigga is not the same anymore. He is obsessed." Taj leaned back in the chair.

"Just be patient with him. Remember he saw him get shot and all that. Ugh! I know I'm sure that is hard to stop seeing. Give him some time." Kalissa urged him.

Taj stood up and stretched. "You wanna smoke one?"

"Nah, but I'll sit outside with you, while you smoke." When Taj looked at her funny, she continued, "You know work tomorrow and that shit just makes me lazy."

"Whateva. Let's go." He walked to the door.

Kalissa grabbed a sweater and walked out behind him. Taj walked down three steps and sat down, while Lissa sat on the top step. When she began talking and he heard the emotion in her voice, he dared not to turn around. He knew how she felt about people seeing her emotional. A definite no-no.

"Things have changed. Not just since Desi died either. All of our life events have changed us in some kind of way. I remember the first time I saw my mom black and blue from a nigga putting his hands on her after she left my dad. It scared me so bad, but really that wasn't what caused me to change. It was when afterwards she had a chance to come back home, to my dad, to us, hell, to me! And she chose to go back to that muthafucka. That's when I knew I would never love a man like that. And I'll never put a nigga before my kids. I was still a kid. I needed my mom, that shit hurt and changed me." Past hurt and anger clipped her every word.

Taj had never heard that story before, but he wasn't surprised. Kalissa let people know what she wanted them to know about her. Other things she just buried.

"Then just like with you. You changed after your mom put you out and I saw the change after Desi almost immediately. That's why I wish you would just get out. Think about it, Tee, you and Cet are in the streets, but y'all ain't come up in the mud like some of these niggas. They don't have shit to lose because ain't nobody ever cared about them. Period." The volume of her voice increased with every word.

"You always say that and sometimes I think about it, but right now I don't see how. The paper is too good." The sigh that came out of Taj sounded as if it came from his soul. "I never meant for it to be like this, fa real. I just wanted the paper, not nobody getting murked. Anyway, if I stop now, what am I gonna do? UPS ain't paying enough and I'm not about to be killing myself working two to three jobs just to pay bills. Nah, that ain't me."

Inhaling twice to catch all the smoke from his blunt, he waited till it went to his head before blowing out the smoke.

"And what about Nigel? You telling him to get out too? I mean, if y'all are going to be together?"

"Mane, that nigga ain't as deep in it as you. But yeah, I'm hoping to convince him to leave it alone. But we ain't talking about him, we talm about yo' ass." A slight chuckle escaped her.

Taj heard her moving around behind him, then he felt her right behind him.

"I know I've changed. You just don't understand, Lissa. Desi would still be here if I hadn't put him on. I feel like I set Desi up for his death. Eventually, I have to get whoever did it back."

He flinched slightly when he felt her knee in his back. The next he felt was her breath in his ear. "What? You thought I was gonna push you down the stairs?"

Tee couldn't see her face and in his mind he knew she was joking, but a slight dread touched his heart. He relaxed when her heard her chuckle.

"You know I'm just messing with you. A bad joke I know. Anyway, Tee, the Bible says let the dead bury the dead. You can only move ahead, his death ain't yo' fight."

"The Bible might say that but the streets say different." Taj cocked his head.

"Not really. These niggas going around killing folks will get handled by the streets. You can't fight for the dead and living at the same time. Somebody is gonna come up short and it will be the living, cuz you too mad about the dead."

"How the fuck the dead going to take care of the folks that's out here just living after they done put somebody in the dirt?"

"The way I see it, vengeance don't belong to us for the dead. They'll sort that shit out. These grimy ass niggas that's out here killing folks for sport or some kind of street cred? They dead anyway! They may walk among us, but eventually they'll get theirs. I promise you they will."

"I hear ya, but I don't agree wit ya." Taj was lost in his anger about Desi's death. "If I didn't do anything I wouldn't have the respect. You a woman, so I don't expect you to understand. Without respect out here, I might as well get a nine to five."

Kalissa's knee dug harder into his back. "Respect from who? The streets don't respect nobody. Most of them niggas waiting for you to fall so that they can take yo' place! Mane, you done let them niggas get in yo' head. Ain't no such thing as respect and loyalty in these streets. Just a bunch of niggas trying to get rich quick and waiting for somebody to fall so they can get their money. You know this, mane."

"That ain't really true. My unc' have respect and loyalty. He came up in the streets," Taj shot back.

"Dude! Yo' unc' came up in a different time, with different rules. And the respect he has came from the community. All his businesses and the way he gives back to the community. If anything happens to him there would be too much heat. And he has people working for him all over the state of Alabama. People know if they come for him, they gonna have an army to fight. Even with all of that I bet he still doesn't have the loyalty you think he does. He has respect and fear, that's it." Lissa's breath was on his ear as she spoke in hushed tones.

Her knees speared his back again as she continued. "You, Cet, Rod and hell, even Nigel, y'all don't have that. If anything happens to one of you, it's just going to be another 'drug-related homicide', and nobody other than the people who love y'all will care. You need to wake up fa real."

Taj heard the emotions in her voice but he didn't want to hear that shit. Without turning his head, he felt her stand up again.

"Bruh, I ain't about to stay out here with you all night, I'm going to bed," Kalissa said.

"I know. But we cool, right?"

"This time. Just don't try that shit again," Lissa laughed.

Taj stood and walked up the stairs to give her a hug. She felt frail and smaller than ever. Once he made it down two steps, her voice stopped him.

"Oh yeah, Tee, you about to be an uncle again," she said non-chalantly.

"Fa real? Damn, Lissa. Are you ha—"

"You just remember what I said. We'll talk soon," she cut him off, holding her hand up.

Taj should have known something was going on with her. Not drinking or smoking and she never asked him about Duke.

Chapter Eight

Kalissa heard Nigel come in after one in the morning. He and Rod had gone to Florida to pick up a package from a new supplier they found. That's why she didn't say anything to Taj for fear that he would tell his uncle.

As much as she didn't like the way Nigel got his money, she had to admit that it had its perks. Plus, they had a baby on the way now, and she was tired of struggling. The good part was that Nigel promised to get a job soon, so that the only work he would continue to do was runs out of town. Kalissa could live with that.

Somehow, the sound of him pissing in the bathroom was comforting to her. It just felt good to have a man that wanted to spend time with her and wasn't running as soon as he heard *baby*. Like Terry had done.

"Damn, I'm tired," Nigel said, as he sat on the side of the bed.

"Did it go okay?" Lissa moved closer to him, craving his body heat.

The muscle on the side of Nigel's jaw was ticking like crazy. "Yeah, Florida went okay. But who the hell you had over here last night?"

"Huh? Nobody but Taj. He came by to apologize and we sat outside and talked." Kalissa figured being outside talking was better than the inside.

"Umm-hmm. I don't like that nigga being over here when I ain't here." Nigel still hadn't smiled, and that muscle still ticked.

"Now you know me and Taj been friends forever, don't even trip like that," Kalissa retorted dismissively.

"Oh, you want to play those games. You ain't fooling me. I know you and that nigga used to fuck, probably still are." He jerked away from her.

"Wait a minute! How the hell you gonna say some shit like that? You think I fuck every man I know? Is that what you trying to say?" Lissa's nostrils flared as suddenly she didn't need his heat, because she was hot.

"I said what I meant. Yo' ass probably have. I don't know," Nigel shrugged as he stood.

"I know damn well you didn't. Just 'cause you fuck friends, fat ass ones at that, don't try to put that shit on me."

Before she could stop it, her foot flew out and kicked him in his ass. Jumping up, she pushed him as hard as she could while he tried to catch his balance. Nigel, still standing, mushed her on her head so hard her butt hit the floor.

"You done fucked up now," she roared, jumping up.

Nigel put his hand out to stop her as he tried to make it to the door. Kalissa grabbed the back of his tee shirt as he made his exit, and she hung on for dear life even as she heard it rip. Nigel made it out the bedroom and to the front door quickly. The front door slammed as she stood in the hallway, still holding onto the piece of his shirt.

With her chest heaving and out of breath, Lissa was too mad to cry. The anger that roared through her body wanted her to scream, but she didn't want to wake up Jamila. So, instead, she went to her closet and began throwing all of Nigel's clothes in the middle of the floor.

***

Nigel pulled over at the nearest gas station and opened the trunk of his car. Inside was an array of clothing. He picked through it until he found the shirt he was looking for. Lissa had scratched his back pretty good, but he felt no pain, only anger. Deep down, he knew that she and Taj were just friends, but that nigga didn't have no business coming around when he wasn't there. Nigel had seen the way Taj looked at Lissa, and not only that; he was jealous of their friendship.

Dabbing a little cologne on, Nigel headed to the one spot he knew was open and where he could blow off some steam. Club Laicos.

The parking lot was full, which didn't say a lot considering the club was small. One way in and one way out. Nigel scrapped his candy stick on the asphalt to put it out. The coke from Florida was a whole lot more potent than what they got from here. Just like Nigel liked it.

Nigel paused at the door, to let a couple exit. As soon as he entered and his eyes adjusted to the dim interior laced in smoke, he felt a tap on his shoulder.

"Where you been hiding?" Sha asked as she moved in closer.

Nigel sucked in his teeth before he turned around. Shatoria— or Sha, as she liked to be called—was a hoe that he used to mess around with, when he needed a place to lay his head. She had on a sleeveless one-piece purple sequin dress to match her purple contacts. Her blond weave hung down her back, offsetting her ensemble.

"What up, ma? You looking good." Nigel gave her a half hug.

"You still didn't answer my question. You been dodging a bitch and leaving me on read. What's up wit' you?" Sha wrung her neck and stood with her hands on her hips, toes pointed in together to accentuate the gap between her legs.

"Just been busy. Why you questioning a nigga as soon as he walk through? Damn! You must miss this dick." Nigel smiled at her.

"Nigga, please! I don't never have to miss no dick, I don't know who you think you is." Sha tried to brush past him.

As he watched the bottom of her ass cheeks hang from beneath her short dress, he followed behind her.

"Hold up, ma. Let me buy you a drink or two," Nigel yelled as he caught up with her.

"Now you talking! I guess I can forgive yo' ass," she laughed.

After a few drinks with Sha dancing in her seat, she began to look better. Sha wasn't the best looking, but she liked to party and gave good head. Nigel rearranged his dick in his pants. Then she started talking.

"You remember the last time I saw you?"

"Nah, baby. I know it's been a while, but like I said I been busy," Nigel answered.

"Oh, so you trying to act like you don't remember when you dissed me in the club? When you was with that stuck up looking bitch?" Sha was wringing her neck again.

Nigel leaned across the table and looked her deep in her eyes. "That's how it goes. You know how to play your role, don't you?"

"Nigga, you must have me mixed up!" she sputtered.

Nigel put his hand under the table and rubbed her thigh, sliding his hand close to her pussy.

"Why don't we go to yo' place and you can show me what that mouth do?"

Sha's dimples showed as she tried not to smile. "I knew you missed this pussy. You gonna mess around and one day you won't be able to get it." She sassed while getting up.

Nigel got up and draped his arm around her waist. As they walked, he cupped one butt cheek in his hand. He was too drunk to notice a phone pointed his way, furiously taking pictures.

Once out in the parking lot, Nigel clicked the key fob to unlock his Jeep. "Get in, I got to piss right quick."

Sha settled in the Jeep and looked around. Glancing in the back, she noticed a doll on the floor and a pink shirt or sweater. *This nigga trying play house and think he gonna treat me like a hoe*, Sha thought. Keeping her eyes on his back as Nigel pissed, she grabbed a tube of lipstick out of her clutch and threw it under his seat. Moving quickly as she heard him finishing, she pulled her oversized hoop earring off and slid it on the side of her seat.

Nigel got in and lit up his blunt, looking at her with a smile.

"You should have left your dick out, baby," Sha said coyly.

"Shidd, you ain't said nothing but a word." Nigel balanced the blunt in his mouth while working his dick out.

With a grin she leaned over the console, ignoring the emergency brake poking her and, just as she expected, he was hard as a rock.

Sha opened her mouth wide and almost swallowed him whole, letting her spit build up in her mouth. Lowering her tongue, she inhaled him to the back of her throat.

"Damn, baby! You gonna make a nigga wreck," Nigel moaned, steering with one hand and pushing her head down with the other.

It only took five minutes to get her place. Sha lived in a duplex two blocks away from the club. Nigel jumped out with his dick still hanging out, ready to fuck. Sha teetered on her high heels to her front door when he remembered his condoms were in the console. Sha gave great head, but she already had three kids, and he still remembered when she burned him a year ago.

Before he walked in the door, his last thought was: *Fuck Lissa.*

C.D. Blue

Chapter Nine

Lissa slept fitfully throughout the rest of the night. Actually, she didn't sleep very much at all. Each time she heard a car pull up in her parking lot, she peeped out of the window, hoping it was Nigel. After a few hours, she figured he was out with another woman. Probably Fefe!

Unable to hold her eyes or the blinds open any longer, she drifted off to sleep.

There was a roaring in her ears. Her grandmother stood in a red fitted dress that flowed freely at the bottom on white sand with the bluest water and skies behind her.

"Kalissa, don't open your heart and close your eyes. Reacting strictly from emotions will do you no good. You have been blessed with looks and intelligence. Looks alone will get you in the door and maybe a seat at the table. Using twenty percent of your looks and eighty percent of your intelligence will enable you to own every place you enter. Think more, speak less, don't give all of your heart and trust to anyone. That's when you will become a QUEEN.

The roaring stopped, and only sounds of birds tweeting their sweet song was left in her ears.

Kalissa jumped up, realizing that the damn birds happened to be her alarm clock. Rushing around to get herself and Jamila ready for work and school, it didn't escape her that Nigel hadn't made it home. That cut like a knife in an open wound. As Jamila sat at the table eating her oatmeal, Kalissa grabbed two trash bags and put Nigel's clothes in them. Leaving them at the bedroom door, she put her game face on, walked to the front to gather her baby and start her day.

It was a long day. Kalissa spent most of her time peeping at her phone. This nigga hadn't even called her! Fear snaked up her spine. What if something had happened to him and here she was mad?

That notion was dispelled when an hour before she was scheduled to get off, her phone vibrated in her pocket. It was

Nigel. Lissa's anger came back with a vengeance as she decided not only not to answer, but also not to call him back.

It ticked her off so bad, Kalissa decided not to go home. Instead, she picked Jamila up and headed to her sister, Mahali's house. Her sister lived in a cul-de-sac in east Montgomery, the area most people with money lived. Mahali always kept her house up, nails and hair done, usually with the help of some man. Her daughter, Dawn, was three years older than Jamila and the spitting image of her mother.

Hey, chile, what you got going on?" Mahali smiled as she answered the door.

One thing about her sister was that she loved having company. After swooping Jamila up in a bear hug and kissing her all over her face, she put her down. Dawn grabbed Jamila's hand and led her to the back.

"You want something to eat?" Mahali asked while walking towards the kitchen.

Lissa began shaking her head until the aromas from heaven hit her nose. Mahalia loved to cook, and did it very well.

"Come on. I got pot roast, potatoes, mustard greens, macaroni and cheese, with cornbread muffins to top it off."

"It smells good. But why so much? Are you expecting company?" Lissa felt bad she hadn't asked that before coming. Manners weren't exactly her forte.

"Girl, no! I just cook like this maybe twice a week, so that I can have something to take to work to eat. You know them damn folks only give us thirty minutes, so it's not like I can go anywhere. Sit down. I'll fix your plate."

Kalissa sat on the bar stool around the island in the kitchen. While Mahali moved around the kitchen, Kalissa looked around. Her sister's place could be featured in any Home magazine. She had the copper pots hanging down from the ceiling, every dish cloth and towel was perfectly synchronized to match. All of her appliances matched, including the microwave, and her kitchen floor was spotless. The glass plate hit the ceramic finish with a clang.

"You want a beer?" Mahali asked from the fridge with two in her hand.

"Nah, I'll take some juice or something," Lissa muttered around her fork.

Eyebrows raised, Mahali just nodded and came back with her beer and Capri Sun for Lissa.

"Really? This is what you call juice?" Kalissa laughed while trying to stick the tiny straw through the hole.

"Hey, other than Dawn, we grown over here. That's her juice. The wine and beer belong to me. Speaking of which, let me fix your baby a plate."

The food was so good, and Kalissa hadn't realized how hungry she was until she began eating. By the time her sister got Jamila settled with a plate in the den, Lissa had gotten up and helped herself to another plate. A smaller version.

Before her sister's butt hit her stool, she dropped a bomb on her.

"I think Nigel's cheating on me."

Confusion and concern immediately lined Mahali's face. "What? No! That man loves you. I can see it in his face."

A lump was forming in Lissa's throat, but she still rolled her eyes. Mahali had only seen her and Nigel together a handful of times. Not enough for her to see all this love she claimed to have seen.

"He didn't come home last night. Then he didn't call me until this afternoon!" The lump had turned into tears that ran down Kalissa's face.

Rising from her place at the island, Mahali grabbed her plate and came back with a napkin. Lissa patted her face.

"Maybe he was working."

Leave it to my sister to make an excuse for a man! Lissa thought.

"He was but then we had an argument."

"Wait! Tell me the whole story," Mahali snapped.

So Kalissa did. The confusion and worry on Mahali's face turned into understanding. Still standing, she leaned over the island.

"Girl, you have to understand, Nigel is not Terry, thank God. Anyway, while Terry would say he was okay with Taj being there, he wouldn't be. He just wouldn't have the balls to say anything. Men from the streets are different. They don't want their 'homies' telling them that their woman had another man over when they aren't there. Speaking of which, when did he move in?" Mahali walked around, motioning with her beer for Lissa to follow. She sat comfortably on the sofa.

"He hasn't moved in, for real, but he's always there. And he'll tell me if he's not going to be there for the night."

"Umm-hmm, well, anyway, maybe it's best that you stick to what you have always done and leave the street niggas alone. Because being out all night and him running across a chicken head or two is all part of the game." Her sister clasped her fingers together and smacked her lips.

"So, you're telling me to just accept this?" Kalissa looked at her in amazement. She would have been better off going to sleep and getting advice from her grandmother in her dreams.

"I'm telling you that is part of that lifestyle. As long as he loves you and takes care of all your needs," she made a suggestive face, "you know and financially, just chill a lil' bit."

This conversation had dried all of Kalissa's tears. There was a frown on her face, but she didn't respond.

Mahali scooted closer. "Think of it like this. If he's paying bills, buying you and Jamila nice things, there will be some things that you just have to overlook. Don't sweat the small stuff."

Unable to hold her tongue any longer, Lissa lashed out. "Nah, that sounds like bullshit to me. You're telling me to be okay with my man fucking other people as long as I get the money? Phhffft, that is a big load shit, Mahali, and you know it!"

"You just think he cheated or did you see him? All I'm saying, is there are certain things that come with that lifestyle and if you can't handle it—" Mahali splayed her hands out in front of her.

"Then you might need to go back to what you are used to. But them niggas cheat too and don't bring nearly as much money to the table."

Kalissa looked around her sister's house and knew that all of her nice things did not come from her income alone. She also knew that most of the time her sister was alone and probably lonely, because she accepted that lifestyle over how she was treated.

"Humph, that's going to be hard too now, because I'm pregnant," Kalissa admitted.

"Say what? Pregnant? You are just full of surprises today. Damn! I guess you are kinda stuck."

"Not me! Just like I have done fine with one, I can do fine with two. I'm not going to be alright wit' any nigga cheating on me. Period!" The emotions she was feeling made Lissa's words come out harsher than she intended.

"Hey, don't get mad at me for trying to school you on life. Two kids are much harder than one. If he wants to be a part of his child's life, plus he's great with Jamila, you're willing to lose that because of a few flaws?"

Did this heifer just call cheating a flaw? Kalissa shook her head at the thought. She loved her sister and came to her because they had a stronger bond than the rest of her family. But this was obviously the wrong topic.

"All righty, I guess I need to go home. Thanks for listening to me and feeding me," Kalissa smiled as she stood.

"You know I'm here for you. Just remember what I said and don't go listening to them pissy tailed friends of yours. They can't keep a man and shouldn't be giving any advice," Mahali chuckled. "And don't be trying to fight while you're pregnant, either!"

Kalissa's eyes bulged, but she kept her lips shut. It was definitely time to go home.

C.D. Blue

Chapter Ten

Taj, Cet, Rod and Rollo pulled up almost simultaneously. All the men had been summoned to the home of James Rivers. James was Taj's uncle and the head of the drug trade within Montgomery and the surrounding smaller towns. Whenever he called, there were no excuses as to not show up.

Taj got out of his vehicle and waited for Cet to get out of his car. Rod and Rollo were dapping each other up on the other side of the street, looking like night and day. Both men were dark and actually could have passed for relations, but that's where the resemblance ended. Rollo was always neat, not flashy, but anybody could tell he had money. Rod was always casual, in jeans, tee shirt and ball cap. Taj was surprised that Nigel hadn't joined Rod. Cet was his right-hand man, so whatever was so urgent, he figured that he needed to hear it first-hand.

"What up, mane?" Rod said, when he walked up to Taj.

"You got it," Nigel responded, nodding at him and Rollo.

"You know what this is all about?" Rollo had slid beside the two men silently.

"Nah, we just got the call to meet. I didn't know y'all was coming," Taj said slowly.

Cet finally got out of the car, and they all walked slowly to the front door. Taj had an idea that they had been summoned about the damage they did in Tuskegee.

James opened the door before they rang the bell. He scowled at all the men as he ushered them into his den. Despite wearing a plain blue tee that had seen better days with a pair of jeans, James was still a formidable sight. He directed the men to sit on the sectional with a wave of his hand, while he sat in his recliner across from them.

"What the hell went on in Tuskegee?" James said without any preamble.

Rod looked down, Taj blew out a breath, Cet looked on defiantly, while Rollo's demeanor never changed.

"Unc', we had to fire back at them niggas that drew on Desi and Duke," Taj stated defensively.

"Wait a minute! When did this shit happen and why am I just hearing about it?" James sputtered with a look of disbelief.

Cet explained, "They went to sell some shit at a party and these niggas pulled up and drew on them. Wasn't no shots fired, but right after that somebody caught us slipping."

"We just needed them niggas to know that we don't play that shit, that's all," Taj finished.

James rubbed his hands together and looked off into the distance before he spoke. "Shit, then I didn't know shit about it until that nigga Tank called me. I thought when the youngin got shot it was a wrong place, wrong time thing. I didn't know there was a beef. You was in this too?" He directed the last question to Rollo.

"Naw, this my first hearing about it. If I had known, I would have been gang wit' it, though. But you wouldn't have known, cuz dead niggas don't talk." Rollo had leaned back into the cushy sofa.

James gave Rollo a sideways glance but addressed Taj. "Why the hell was y'all selling in 'Skegee anyway?"

"Unc', you know we handle the college crowd. We have the weed and pills. Them niggas just be selling blow and rocks. We didn't think it would be an issue. We was just dealing wit' the college parties, and somebody tole them niggas. They was mad cuz we was making money, we wasn't stepping on their toes." Taj shrugged.

"Shit, this nigga came at me like y'all went blazing for no reason at all. Shit, Taj! Why didn't you come to me?"

"Just selling product like we 'posed to do." Taj shrugged.

"No disrespect, James, but we put our crews together to handle it. One, to make sure them niggas knew that we didn't play that shit. Two, so that Taj's crew wouldn't think he was soft and gonna let one of his men get killed without him taking care of it," Rod spoke in his quiet, authoritative way.

This logic seemed to resonate with James. He rubbed the stubble on his chin while he thought about Rod's words.

"I can understand that, it's all part of this life, but two thangs. One, they didn't kill Lil' Desi and this wasn't the right time for this," James spoke slowly, giving Rod, Taj and Cet a hard look.

"Mane, this some bullshit!" Cet jumped up, emotional. "My lil' cuz was shot down like a dog. We didn't hurt nobody cuz we wasn't sure if they did it, but we had to send a message, cuz them niggas drew on us. It was the right time."

Cet spit the knowledge that Rod gave him, like it was his own. Rod sat looking like a proud father, but when Cet jumped up, Taj noticed Rollo's hand went to his piece. Taj stood in front of Cet and got him to sit down. Taj's nerves settled when Rollo spoke:

"Jay, man, he's right. When niggas want to show off and whip out them sticks as a scare tactic, you have to show them that it ain't cool. Big Tank been in the game long enough to know this, mane! I heard a few of 'em got skinned up, but hey, if Big Tank can't handle that maybe he need to step out of the game, with his fat ass."

James rubbed the stubble on his chin, in deep thought. "That's what I'm saying. Humph, this might work out. Lissen up and what I'm bout to tell y'all don't leave this room. I been wanting to get to that area, because along with the college and the casino up the road, there's money to be made. Them niggas just ain't taking advantage of it." James looked at all of them, his gaze stopping at Rollo. "Tank didn't want me to be his distributor, so he started buying from Waski. Dumb muthafucka didn't realize that I supply Waski too." He pulled a cigarette out of the pack, but didn't light it. His wife did not play about smoking inside the house. "But I'm not Waski's only supplier. If we get that area completely, it won't be long before we have expanded to the Georgia line. That's what you call growth." A big smile covered his face.

"Jay, mane, let me handle it. I been knowing them niggas. I'll talk to Tank and get some straightening," Rollo said, looking animated.

James stood and paced from the sofa to the fireplace mantle. "Hmm, don't go too hard, cuz we gonna need some of Tank's men, the ones that know the lay of the land."

"Depends on what that nigga say. He'll decide whether he gets it hard or soft. As far as taking over, most of his crew junkies, that's why they asses can't move shit." Rollo's deep, but soft voice filled the room.

The other three men watched this exchange in silence as James and Rollo locked eyes.

James finally broke the silence. "A'ight, and I figure out something about Waski. He ain't going to be happy about being cut out of the picture."

Once again James and Rollo looked at each other, and Rollo gave a slight nod.

"Y'all niggas get out of here! I need to smoke and y'all asses need to make us some money," he chuckled. James's mood had changed drastically from when they first arrived.

Before they got to the door, Uncle James stopped Taj. "Nephew, next time let me know how you moving. It's some good that came from it, but I don't need you putting yo'self in the line of fire like that. It could've been handled differently."

"I hear ya, Unc'." Taj let out the breath he hadn't realized he'd been holding in.

Rollo and Rod stood at the curb in deep conversation. Taj stopped Cet in the middle of the driveway.

"See, this what make me mad about Unc'. He wants me to tell him my every move. I don't like that shit! He need to let me loose," Taj whispered.

Cet looked towards the street and shrugged. "I feel ya, my nigga, but you have to appreciate what he do, too. You know he got those connections with MPD, that's how we able to move. And he tells us when things are hot. We need that. And this is going to be mo' money for us."

Glancing toward the curb, Taj lowered his voice, "Mane it's something about Rollo. I don't know if I trust that nigga."

With his eyes toward the sky, Cet answered, "He ain't no snake or nothing, he just all business. And I tole you he crazy. Fa real, fa real. A stone-c," Cet stopped as Rod called them over.

"Mane, I wish y'all had told me about yo' plans, I would have been down. And it would've went different," Rollo started as soon as they walked over. "Well, actually, it wouldn't have been, unless y'all just wanted to get at that niggas for drawing on y'all. I could've told you they didn't kill yo' cuz."

Cet hopped in front of Rollo. "How you know? You heard something?"

A chuckle escaped from Rollo. "Mane, them niggas drew on y'all for selling in their spot. Y'all shot up their biggest trap and what did they do? Shit! They called Jay." He shook his head. "Believe me, that ain't no niggas that gonna shoot up yo' shit and kill yo mans."

"That's why we just shot the house up. We ain't hurt nobody, them niggas trying to make it sound like it's more than it was. I hadn't heard nothing in the streets, so we went soft." As Rod spoke up, the toothpick in his mouth was bouncing with every word.

"Yeah, that sound 'bout right." Rollo turned to Cet and Taj "Whoever shot yo' cuz, it will eventually come out. Niggas that won't look you in the eye when they kill ya, will always brag. You just got to stay ready and wait for them to talk to right or wrong one. Get you some ears on the streeet. But you ain't got to worry about them 'Skegee scrubs no mo'. Stay dangerous, my niggas." With a salute, Rollo walked off.

C.D. Blue

Chapter Eleven

Nigel's car was in the parking lot when Kalissa and Jamila pulled up. There was no denying that her heart fluttered with joy when she saw it. The fight they had, totally convincing herself that he was cheating, could not stop the love she had for him. With a deep breath, she braced herself for what was upstairs as she remembered his clothes that she had packed up in trash bags. She was too tired to fight.

"Nigel's here," Jamila's said in a singsong voice, while she struggled to free herself from her car seat.

"Yes, he is," Lissa mumbled under her breath.

Walking in the door, the first thing that hit her was the smell of food. It filled the apartment, along with some old school music. Nigel walked from the kitchen, gave her that devilish grin but before he could say or do anything, Jamila ran to him with a hug.

"Hey, where y'all been?" he asked as he looked under Jamila whom he held in the air.

"At my sister's," Lissa answered with a slight attitude in case he came with the shits.

Before Lissa could make it to the back, her eyes landed on the dining table, which held a vase full of red roses. The anger and attitude melted away. No one had ever given her flowers before, and she felt the burn of tears behind her eyelids.

Then that doggone reminder came back that this nigga had stayed out all night, without calling her or anything. Three blinks, and the tears were gone.

"Come on, Jamila, get ready for your bath and bed, momma has work tomorrow," she interrupted the squeals of fun.

Kalissa had never bathed her daughter so quickly. Of course, that meant that getting in the bed and going to sleep took some time, but eventually Jamila was deep in slumber.

Nigel was sitting on the sofa wide legged, looking at the TV. Kalissa walked in softly but didn't sit down. Instead, she stood looking at him as if there would be some tell-tale sign of his cheating on his face.

"Where were you last night?" She approached the subject timidly.

"I got drunk and stayed at Rod's. Why?" Nigel answered nonchalantly, never looking from the screen.

"Why? Because you didn't come back. That's why? Your ass was probably wit' somebody." The last part slipped out by mistake.

Nigel glanced her way, then took a deep breath. "You always thinking about that kind of shit! I didn't feel like arguing wit' yo' monkey ass, so I didn't come back. Is that a crime?"

Whoa! His response startled her because she just knew he was supposed to begging her for forgiveness at this point.

"I think it's a fair assumption. I mean if I stayed out all night, you would think the same. Hell, I can't even sit on the steps wit' my best friend without you accusing me of fucking him. But if you stay out all night, don't answer my calls, you just do whatever? That's some bullshit!"

"Well, that's what it is. You can take or leave it, Kalissa," Nigel said angrily.

The mad energy drained out of her. Kalissa didn't want to fight, she just wanted Nigel to reassure her that she was all he wanted. That nigga couldn't even do that!

"I'm going to bed." She huffed, looking at him. Pivoted on the ball of her foot, she looked over her shoulder at him. He was back watching television! "And fuck you!"

"Whateva! Before you go to sleep you need to hang my shit back up!" Nigel shot back.

"Nigga-a-a-a, I wish I would," she threw back over her shoulder as she stomped to the bedroom. As soon as she entered the bedroom, the trash bags filled with his clothes greeted her. Lissa kicked one in anger.

Her shower wasn't much help because the water wasn't hot enough, so she couldn't stay in it for her usual twenty plus minutes. The night just got worse when she saw Nigel had moved to the bedroom.

Still stomping, she climbed into the bed purposely with her back to him. Obviously more tired than she realized, she was drifting off until she felt Nigel's dick in her back. Lissa scooted to the edge of the bed.

"Hey, I know you're mad at me, but is yo' pussy mad too?" Nigel whispered while he nudged her back.

Kalissa ignored him, but she couldn't ignore his hands when they started rubbing her back. She tried but when he reached her ass, a moan escaped her. When she tried to roll over, he held her in place.

"Un uh, don't move," Nigel whispered as he slipped inside her wetness.

Tooting her ass up to meet him, it was pure bliss as he slid out slowly far enough for her to feel the ridge of his head.

Tilting forward, he held her hips as they made love to the slow tempo of what their hearts could not contain. Each stroke dimmed her anger slightly until she felt him harden inside of her.

"Damn. Lil' mama, I love you," Nigel rasped as he came.

The tight manner in which he held her, as she felt his seed spurt inside her, killed all the anger and doubt she felt.

"Sorry, that was a quick one. Yo' pussy so good I couldn't stop," he laughed as he released her.

"Hmm mmm," was the only response she gave as she cuddled beside him.

"Don't forget you gonna hang my shit back up in the morning," Nigel whispered in her ear before she drifted off to sleep with a smile on her face.

C.D. Blue

Chapter Twelve

"Come on, girl," Zo moaned to the young lady he was leading into the trap.

"I thought we was going to yo' place," she whined.

"Naw, if you want me to buy you nice things, I have to work. This is my job." Zo smiled at her.

"Yeah, but if you running thangs like you say, why you got to work the trap?" she questioned, still hanging back.

"Like I told you, I'm training with Rollo right now and once I learn everythang, that nigga will be working for me. So, I'm watching the trap for him tonight. You coming or nah?"

The young lady looked hesitant but grabbed Zo's outstretched hand. Zo led her into the trap, sidestepping the takeout containers and paper that lined the floor.

"Damn! Don't they ever clean this place up?" The young lady whose name Zo didn't remember scrunched her nose up.

"Yeah, I got to get these lil' niggas on track. That's what I'm saying, I had to come by here. Cuz these niggas will try anything if I don't check on them. My unc' is depending on me." Zo flowed smoothly.

"Umm-hmm. In my hood they treat Rollo like a king. Everybody get excited when he come through," she said wistfully.

Zo rolled his eyes and put a line of coke on the dinner tray he kept in the bedroom. "Come on, get a lil' sniff of this. This shit right here will make yo' ass forget all about Rollo."

When she bent over, her titties almost fell out of her low-cut shirt. She had dressed just for this occasion. She wanted a baller, and Zo had talked the right shit.

Zo dipped his little finger in his baggie, pulling out the coke on his fingernail. After repeating this a few times, he grabbed a fifty dollar bill out of his pocket and waved at his companion.

When she reached for it, he shook his head and laughed. "Give me some head for it. Show me what you working wit'."

While the young lady moved some trash out of the way to get on her knees, Zo pulled his hard dick out of his pants.

A smile crossed his face as he closed his eyes and guided her head. The loud slurping noise she made was all he could concentrate on.

"Yeah, suck it jus' like that. You must want more than that fiddy," Zo said through clenched teeth. "A lil' mo' spit. That's it, do that shi—"

The cold draft of air hitting his dick cut him off.

"Mane, what the fuck is you doing?" Rollo yelled, holding the young lady by the back of her shirt.

"I was just having a lil' downtime," Zo stuttered, while stuffing his dick back in his pants.

Rollo's mouth twisted in disgust. He gently let go of Zo's friend's shirt. "What's yo' name, lil' princess?"

"Iesha," the young lady said, looking down.

"Look here, Iesha, don't never let a nigga get you on your knees for some money. You deserve respect. And being on yo' knees in some trashy ass room ain't worth it, okay?" Rollo said.

Iesha nodded, visibly trembling in fear. Rollo pulled out a roll of cash and peeled off two one-hundred-dollar bills. He handed them to her.

"Go home, don't ever come back here and remember what I told you. Okay?"

Iesha nodded and tipped through the trash in the room to make it to the door. Once she left the room, she ran through the house to get out.

Zo ran his hand across his face before looking at Rollo. The room was dark but the sliver of light from the hallway allowed Zo to see Rollo's face. He stood still with his hand on his waist. Zo knew that was where his burner was.

"Mane—" Zo started.

"Nigga, as long as you with me, don't you never bring no little girl to the trap. No hoes, period! I'ma give yo' ass a pass this time, because maybe you don't know no better."

"Nigga, I ain't know how old that hoe was," Zo grumbled.

Rollo just looked at him for a minute without saying anything.

"Nigga, a blind man could see that was a kid. I don't know if yo' ass slow or what. Jus' remember what I told you."

Zo jumped up. "Nigga, I ain't slow! I said—"

It felt like steel clamped around his neck as Zo felt his breath leaving him.

"Don't you never run up on me, my nigga. Unless you ready to die, ya heard!"

Rollo pushed him back as he released his neck. Zo gasped for air.

"I called a meeting. You got fifteen minutes to get this place cleaned up. We finished for now, but we ain't done," Rollo said, wiping his hands off on his pants.

Zo sulked out of the room, still rubbing his neck. He mumbled to himself when he saw Rollo's biggest ass kisser, Duck, standing in the hallway. Zo brushed by him, knocking his shoulder into Duck's arm.

"Mane, watch where the fuck you going!" Duck yelled to his back.

***

Rollo and his second-in-command—Duck—rode silently to Tuskegee. They both bopped their heads to the music. Behind them was a SUV five niggas deep, just in case some shit popped off. Duck was always with him when he took care of business. Most of the crew understood because the two men came up together.

"Mane, why you keep dealing wit' that pussy ass nigga back there? That nigga should be stretched for fucking wit' that lil' girl." Duck sounded frustrated.

"Shole ya right, but ya know he's Jay's nephew, so I gave him his last pass. I promised Jay I wouldn't fuck him up, unless he fucking up product or the bands. I ain't know he was Chester the fucking molester. I see why his own fam kicked him out."

Duck's dreads swung from side to side as he listened. Tall and skinny, most people underestimate him because they thought he was a pretty boy. He was light-complexioned and actually had freckles across his face, but he was mean as a snake.

"Shid, wit' what he doing, he gonna get us all fucked up," Duck mumbled.

"Nephew, before I let him do that, I'll give that nigga back to the dirt. I got eyes everywhere. That nigga biggest mistake is that his slow ass think he smart," Rollo responded.

"I don't trust his ass. It's something 'bout that nigga that just rubs me the wrong way," Duck's deep voice filled the car.

"He might be stupid, but he ain't crazy. He either gonna learn the easy way or the hard way. You just stay dangerous."

"Say less, my nigga. You know me, this strap is my number one hoe." A smile sneaked on Duck's face.

Tuskegee Institute was a private HBCU that touted all the famous engineers it produced. You would think that would have made the city lively and growing. Not true. It was still country, with very few businesses and still one of the poorest cities in the state.

Tank's main trap was eight miles west of the college, and the streets were trashy, and all the houses looked to be one good wind away from falling apart. The trap house included.

Taj and Cet had left their mark. Most of the windows were boarded up with plywood, and the old rusted Buick that sat in the front was filled with bullet holes and no windows. The house had one of those high porches but thankfully, the steps were cement. Two dirty old-fashioned tin patio chairs sat on the porch, rust-streaked with the original lime green color.

"Mane, what the fuck is this shit? I thought I heard some of these niggas lived here?" Duck mused aloud.

"They do. So that tells ya right there ain't too much of nothing going on. This should be easy as hell," Rollo answered.

After Rollo knocked, Duck pulled his pants up, while looking around.

"Who da fuck is it?" a gruff voice called out.

A short dark guy with a gold top grill snatched the door open, mean mugging Duck until he saw Rollo.

"What up, mane? I didn't know that was you," he grinned, chopping it up.

"It's cool, no worries. Where Tank at?" Rollo said smoothly, stepping inside.

"He back there in his office. Don't worry 'bout this shit, some lame ass niggas shot us up the other day," the guy motioned to the plywood.

Duck dapped him up. "If I cut my foot, I'ma shoot ya ass."

The top grill's eyes widened until Duck laughed. He laughed nervously with him. After watching them walk to the back, the top grill went and got a broom.

"What up, Tank?" Rollo said loudly as they walked into the 'office'.

"What the f—" Tank was snorting blow from a steak knife, but looked up when he heard Rollo. "What up, Rollo? Who the hell let y'all back here without telling me?" He gave Duck a nod.

"Your mans up front. Ya know, they all know me, so it's cool," Rollo looked around.

"Hump, them muthafuckas act like they ain't got the sense they was born wit'." Tank kept talking while putting the knife on top of the desk. He pulled out his cell phone.

"Yo, Marquis? You and Skeet need to brang yo' asses back here to my office," Tank barked into the phone.

Tank eyed Duck and Rollo suspiciously before his men came in. Both were big, one had cornrows going to the back, the other was bald. They stood at the entrance of the office with their arms crossed. Once they were in place, Tank broke out in a grin.

"I knew somebody would be up here after them fuck boys shot up my place. I shoulda known it would be you," he laughed, looking at his men.

Rollo stood with his arms at his side, while Duck cocked his head to the side.

Tank stood up with his hands splayed on top of the desk. "How much longer you gonna be James' do boy? You ought to be tired of him sending you to clean up shit. I hope he sent you wit' some money, since you want to run his errands. That's why you ain't gonna never be a boss. Fa' real tho'."

One man snickered while the other laughed out loud. Rollo held his fist up to his mouth while he chuckled, showing his deep dimples.

"Yo' man, you funny as hell. Shoulda been a comedian or something," Rollo said with an imperceptible move forward.

Tank shrugged, "It's the truth."

Rollo nodded then snapped his fingers. Everything after that happened quickly. Duck pulled his piece out and shot both men in the head. Rollo made it over to the desk in a flash and stuck the steak knife in Tank's hand.

"Ughhh, nigga!" Tank screamed as blood splashed up in his face.

Rollo put a finger up to his mouth and looked up to the ceiling. "Ya hear that?"

"Hear what, mane?" Tank gasped as beads of sweat lined his forehead.

"Ain't nobody laughing now, is they? You got your man's kilt for some ha-ha, hee-hee shit." Rollo shook his head.

Tank's eyes shut as he heard a groan and a thud on the other side of the door. Duck came around the cheaply made desk and grabbed a .357 and a sawed-off shotgun.

"Ro, I was jus' fucking wit' you, I didn't mean nothing. You didn't have to kill them. Mane, you crazy!" Tank pleaded as he squatted behind the desk in pain.

"And you knew this, mane, but yet you still wanted to be funny," Rollo said, twisting the knife to the left.

Sweat rolled down Tank's face, mixing with tears as he groaned in pain.

"Look, we cool. Can you take this knife out my hand so we can talk?" Tank moaned.

"Nah, nigga. What's wrong wit' yo' tongue?" Rollo smiled dangerously.

"A'ight, look, I don't have no problem working wit' y'all but Waski ain't gonna go for that. And most of my crew might have a problem wit' all this going on," Tank spoke rapidly.

84

"You let us handle Waski and fuck your set. Look like you just killed yo' best ones anyway. But you, nah, we ain't no working together." Rollo furrowed his brow together, before pulling the knife free.

Tank laid his head on the desk before grabbing a towel from the floor, trying to stop the flow of blood.

"You know I was just talking shit, mane. But you can't jus' run me out my spot," Tank muttered, still holding his hand.

Rollo took his nine out and looked at it, then turned it sideways at Tank. Not taking any chances, Tank held his hands up in the air, mindless of the blood flowing down his arm.

"Nah, nigga, it was all fun and games a minute ago. Why yo' big ass ain't laughing now?" Rollo paused and looked at the ceiling.

"I came here to talk business. A partnership. But you don't understand that. Yo' ass snorting shit up yo' nose, getting yo' own fucking crew killed and you think we want to work wit' you?" Rollo scowled as he looked at Tank. "You wanna do this the hard way or the easy way?"

"Fuck this shit! I don't wanna work wit' James ass no way!" Tank huffed, still holding his hand.

"That's cool. Have yo' shit out of here by the end of the week," Rollo said softly.

Rollo and Duck eased out of the room, holding their pieces close to them. They stepped over the body in front of the door. It seemed as if everyone had cleared out, except the top grill who let them in. He held his hands up in front of him.

"There's been a change in management. You riding wit' us?" Rollo asked.

"Hell yeah, I'll ride wit' y'all," he showed his grill before looking towards the office, where Tank stood at the door mean mugging him.

"What's your name?" Duck asked.

"Trev," his smiled dimmed. "What about Tank?"

"Tank will be a'ight. He yo' homeboy from back in the day or some?"

"Nah, I just been wit' him for a few months. I moved here from Valley," Trev said slowly.

"Take my number and go home. Don't come back here until I call you, okay?" Rollo said softly, reciting his number as Trev entered it in his phone. Trev dialed, letting Rollo's phone ring twice, then hanging up.

"Lock me in," Trev requested, as he looked back down the hall, before walking out the door.

"A'ight, Tank, we will see ya soon," Rollo called out.

"Fuck you, nigga," Tank shot back.

By the time they got to the interstate, Rollo glanced over at his partner. Duck nodded to the beat that thumped throughout the vehicle.

"You want me to dead that nigga?" Duck asked.

"Nah, not yet. That nigga don't want this smoke. He jus' frontin'."

Chapter Thirteen

Three Months Later

Malachi looked at the picture on his phone, back to the woman sitting in her car. Almost certain they were one and the same, he couldn't be sure until she got out. His leg bounced with impatience.

Finally, her door swung open and he hopped out, closing the distance between them with a few strides.

"Kalissa?"

The woman stopped in mid-stride and looked back at him from head to toe. Malachi was used to getting looks like that. Towering most women at six-four, a muscular frame, his shiny bald head and neat goatee had that effect. Not to mention his size fourteen feet. Kalissa's glance showed no interest, only suspicion.

"Yeah," she answered, still not turning completely around.

"Sorry to approach you like this, but I'm Malachi, Brian's brother," he said gently, since she looked as if she was ready for flight.

Malachi noticed her stance relaxed slightly, but the suspicion remained in her eyes.

"I hate to bother you at work, but I didn't know any other way to reach you. I'll tell you it's been hard." He smiled, trying to ease the tension.

"Oh well, I'm sorry about Brian," she said simply.

"Yes, it's been rough. That's actually why I'm here. I don't feel as if the police are putting forth much effort to find out. It's driving my mom crazy." Malachi raised both hands.

"I bet," Kalissa murmured.

"I know y'all were talking and I was wondering if you have any idea who could have been that mad at him. Mad enough to kill him and just leave him?" His voice went up an octave at the end. Taking a deep breath, he tried to reel in his anger.

"Uh, I have no idea. I was shocked when I heard the news. I just can't imagine anyone," Kalissa said softly.

With a dramatic drop in his shoulders, Malachi covered his eyes with his hand before swiping it down over his face. He noticed her looking back to the employee entrance of the restaurant.

"I know y'all were dating, so I thought maybe he shared if he was having beef with anyone?"

Kalissa's eyes shifted up above his head, understanding that he asked the same question in a different way. She shook her head. "You know we weren't really speaking when that happened. Even before that, we were just kicking it, nothing serious."

"Hmm, he told me some things. But I don't think he saw it as just kicking it. It's killing me, ya know. I wish I had been with him or at least I could have talked him out of going to look for you at the club." Malachi dropped that information, closely watching her face.

Kalissa's heart went out to him about his brother, but when she heard the last part, her mind went into overdrive.

"Why would you think he was looking for me at the club?" she asked, her voice rising an octave.

"That's what he told one of his homeboys," Malachi's eyes never left her face.

Other than slightly narrowing her eyes, her expression didn't change. "That's weird. I've never heard that before. I wonder why he thought I would be there. But anyway, I don't think I was there, but I know that any time I've gone to that club, I never saw him there."

"Not sure. I'm not leaving Montgomery until I find out what happened. It's tearing my family apart and I talked to club owners, but they don't have working cameras. The police say they have no witnesses. Nobody knows what he was doing out back, it's just crazy." Malachi went off on tangent without taking his eyes off Kalissa.

"I'm sure. I'm sorry I can't help you. I need to get in to clock in, sorry," she said, quickly looking at her phone.

"I understand. Can I give you my number? Just in case you think of anything or hear anything?" He pulled his phone out.

88

"Umm, sure. What's your number?" When Kalissa held her phone out to take his number down, her windbreaker opened.

"Oh shit! Are you pregnant? And is it—" Malachi exclaimed.

The first real smile appeared on her face since they had been talking. "Yeah, I am." Her smile faltered. "But no, it's not Brian's." Frown wrinkles appeared in between her brows.

"Oh. I'm sorry. It just caught me off guard." Malachi rattled off his number.

Kalissa asked him to repeat, as she punched it in. "You live in Birmingham?"

"Nah, I was in Mobile. I'm here now until I get this squared away."

"Oh. I'm sorry about what happened to Brian, but it was nice to meet you." Her face went through the seemingly appropriate measures: a sad look followed by a slight smile.

"Same here. I'm sure I'll see you again soon," he said meaningfully.

Kalissa turned on her heel and walked quickly to the restaurant.

***

Kalissa's heart felt as if it was coming out her chest. There were only a few people at work. A small crew in the kitchen prepping, along with the kitchen manager and one of the dishwashers. While clocking in, she kept her eyes on the parking lot. Malachi had made it to a sleek sports car, but instead of getting in, he seemed to be looking around the parking lot. Kalissa made taking her jacket off and hanging it up a slow process, still watching out the window.

"Hey, Sheila called and said she would be a little late," the kitchen manager said, walking behind her.

"Shit, you scared me!" Lissa yelled after her entire body flinched. "Okay, that's fine."

"I'm sorry, I called yo' name, I guess you didn't hear me," he chuckled, walking off.

Who the hell knew Brian even had homeboys? Or a brother? was her main thought as she took her phone into single restroom in the back.

As soon as the door closed, she locked it and leaned against it, closing her eyes. In her mind Kalissa ran through many conversations she had with Brian. Once he did tell her that he had a brother, but all she could remember was that he was six or seven years older. Her hands shook so bad she had to dial the number three tries before the call went through.

"We have a problem," was her greeting.

"What's going on now?" Nigel said in response.

Kalissa told him about her morning visitor and what he said.

"Shit! A'ight, lil' mama, don't worry, I'll call Rod. We'll see you when you get off. And Lissa! Don't talk to his ass if he come back up there," Nigel warned.

"Okay, I won't." Lissa could hear the wind sounds of the car, and she knew that Nigel was dropping Jamila off at the daycare. Usually, that made her smile, but she could not fake the funk.

With a slight tug she grabbed one paper towel, throwing it away, then pulling two more from the dispenser. Her hand shook as she ran cold water over it. Dabbing her face, she washed her hands, sprayed air freshener and smoothed down her shirt before opening the door.

Phyliss, one of the prep cooks, stood three feet away from there, looking at her curiously.

"You alright, baby? I was about to come check on you. Is you still having morning sickness?"

Kalissa managed a smile. "No, but I had to do a little more than pee. I'm okay."

"Oh honey! I know how that is. Them babies will have yo' body doing all kind of crazy stuff. You just take it easy, okay?" Phyliss said cheerfully.

"Yes, ma'am, I will," Kalissa answered before she walked to the front. It was surprising that she hadn't shit on herself. She was scared. Not police scared. No matter how smooth Malachi spoke or how he dressed, if Kalissa got close enough, she could always tell a street nigga. That nigga was street!

It was the longest day ever! Kalissa alternated between watching the clock and looking out into the parking lot. An hour before the end of her shift, she stood in the front with her back to the door as she sent Nigel a text, letting him know what time she would be home.

"Excuse me, miss, can I just go to the bar?" a man said to her back.

The voice sounded familiar, and she was just glad it wasn't Brian's brother. When she turned, she saw Rollo standing in the foyer. Alone, as usual.

"Hey, lil' sis!" Rollo had started calling her that ever since he knew she and Nigel were together.

"Hey, bro, what's up?" Kalissa was glad to see him, and also wondered if Nigel or Rod had sent him there.

"What? You 'bout to give me a niece or nephew? Damn, I'm always the last to know." Rollo chuckled. "I didn't even know you worked here. I ain't never seen you here before."

Kalissa smiled. "Yep, I sure am. You must come at night, cuz I've been here for a while."

"Yeah, I usually do. That's what's up. Tell Nigel I'll holla at him soon," Rollo said before he strolled to the bar.

Kalissa watched him as he dapped it up with the bartender, then he began watching one of the televisions above the bar. She liked Rollo because he always seemed about business. The few times she had seen him, he never hung around anywhere too long, nor did he ever say anything slick about how they met. He was cool.

The bar area was empty except for Rollo and a lady that sat across from him, giving him the eyeball. Kalissa walked over.

"Hey, is Zo still with you?" she asked innocently as she sat on the stool next to him, keeping her eye on the door.

"If that's what you wanna call it. Yeah, that fool wit' me." Rollo rolled his eyes and laughed. Holding his drink up, he cut his eyes at Kalissa before taking a sip. "You know that nigga?"

"Umm-hmm, we went to school together." She saw a car pull up in the parking lot. "Whateva you do, don't trust that nigga," she told Rollo, sliding off the stool.

"Hold up, sis! You can't drop a gem and leave without giving the knowledge." Rollo grabbed her arm.

Kalissa tore her eyes away from the door and looked dead in his face. "I gotta go. Just know that he's grimy, a thief and a liar. He just ain't shit, that's all. You can't trust him wit' nothing!"

Rollo leaned back, his eyes taking her in. "I gotcha, sis. I peeped that kinda of early on, but you just confirmed my thoughts. I 'preciate ya."

Kalissa nodded, then gave him a one arm hug before meeting the two customers at the door.

Chapter Fourteen

Nigel and Rod were at her apartment by the time she arrived home. After giving them both a hug, she went to shower and change. The worry was evident in Rod's eyes, but Nigel seemed fine. Or at least he was better at hiding how he felt.

After changing, she walked back up front, where Jamila sat in the middle of the floor with her Barbie dolls.

"Hey, I'm going to get something to eat. Then after I put her in the bed, we can talk," Kalissa said with a glance at her daughter.

"Momma, you can talk before I go to bed," Jamila chimed in.

That broke the tension as they all laughed. Finding out what they wanted, Nigel stopped her before she left. He threw his keys.

"Here, take my truck," Nigel said.

Jamila wanted to go to the fast food joint with her mom. After getting her in the truck, in her car seat, one of her shoes fell off. When Kalissa reached for it, something sparkly caught her eye. It was an earring! And not one of hers!

Kalissa's stomach did flip flops, and her chest became tight. Her eyes traveled back up to the apartment and it took all of her willpower not to go back up there.

Before she made it to the fast food restaurant, she stopped at the gas station and looked around the car. Tears stung her eyes when she found the tube of lipstick, and her heart dropped when she found condoms in the center console, with two missing.

"Momma, I thought we were going to get something to eat?" Jamila's little voice broke through her fog.

"We are. Right now," she managed to croak past the huge lump in her throat.

When they made it back to the house, she glared at Nigel and slid the bag of food across the coffee table. Nigel and Rod glanced at each other, with Rod raising his brows and Nigel answered with a shrug.

Jamila talked through her meal, Kalissa picked through hers, but Rod and Nigel ate theirs with no problem.

"Lil' mama, what's wrong wit' you?" Nigel yelled across the room.

"Nothing," she mumbled.

"Well, get me a beer then, since ain't nothing wrong wit' ya," Nigel said jokingly.

"Get yo' own beer, I'm about to give Jamila a bath," Kalissa snapped.

"I got you, mane. You know yo' wifey tired, damn, you trying to work her after she get off work," Rod chuckled as he got up with his trash in his hand.

Kalissa left her food on the table, as she took her daughter to the back to bathe her and get her in bed. Their nightly routine included a story and Kalissa laying with her until she fell asleep.

"What's wrong, momma?" Jamila asked, rubbing her hand across Kalissa's face.

As heavy as her heart was, she managed a smile. Jamila was so close to her mom, it was if she could see through her.

"Nothing, baby, just tired. Hey, do you want a little brother or sister?"

"No, I don't think so," Jamila said, snuggling close to Kalissa's chest.

Kalissa pulled her close with a chuckle. Once her daughter's breathing was steady, the tears fell from her eyes effortlessly. All that she could think about was the night Nigel stayed out. Then other thoughts invaded her mind: The time he had during the day when she was at work, women who looked better and had better shapes, who were also possibly more fun. A burning sensation ran through her body as the tears fell harder. Once believing what she wanted to believe instead of what was right in her face, the reality of the situation slapped her again. Kalissa closed her eyes, hoping that would stop the stream of tears, and the image of Brian's brother appeared behind her eyelids.

A deep breath shuddered through her body as she wiped her face with Jamila's sheet. The first stop was the bathroom, to pee and run cold water over her face. The cold water didn't help until she splashed some in each eye. That took most of the redness out.

Rod sat in the chair, and Nigel was on one side of the sofa. Kalissa sat on the opposite end, without looking at him.

"Aye, so what did ole boy say to you?" Rod got right to the point.

Kalissa cleared her throat and sat up straighter. She relayed the entire conversation and when she got to the part about Malachi knowing she was at the club, Nigel did the weirdest thing. He leaned over and licked her cheek, then gave her a smile and a wink. Her heart tried to melt, but she thought about those condoms and rolled her eyes.

Rod rubbed his chin, got up and began to pace. "That's fucked up. Does he look like the type to go to the five-o?"

"He was trying to look that part, but no. I'm pretty sure he isn't that type," Kalissa looked down at her hands.

"I don't know, mane, maybe we should tell James and see what he thinks we should do," Rod said, sitting back down.

Kalissa's head snapped up. "James? Why do you want to do that?"

"I mean, he knows police officers or maybe he can handle it one way or the other," Rod said.

"True, dat. James would be able to handle it without a problem," Nigel piped in.

"That doesn't sound like a good idea. Nobody else needs to know. Did y'all tell somebody what happened?" Kalissa looked from one man to the other.

Both of them shook their heads.

"Well, I haven't either and I think it should stay that way. Involving James would add one more person, then if he wants to handle it, there go some more people finding out, the next thing you know we all in jail. Nope, as long as we don't talk about it, you know, to y'all's girlfriends and shit," she paused and looked at Nigel, "we should be okay. And nobody else gets hurt. Make sense?"

Rod gave her an odd look before slowly nodding. "Yeah, when you put it like that. Makes sense, but I don't think he's just going to go away. I wouldn't if it was my brother."

Kalissa looked at him in amazement, all types of slick remarks passing through her brain. Instead, she got up and went to the table, cleaning it off while she tried to think of something decent to say.

"He probably won't, but he also won't be able to find anything out either. I just hope I never see him again." A shudder went through her body.

"A'ight, let me know if you do. I'm out, y'all," Rod said, stepping to Kalissa first for a hug, then Nigel.

Nigel stood and stretched. "What did you mean by *y'all's girlfriends*? You always got some slick shit coming out yo' mouth."

"Really? What about the condoms in yo' truck? Don't that mean yo' ass got a girlfriend?" She pointed at her bulging stomach. "Cuz obviously we don't use them."

A myriad of expressions crossed Nigel's face. "That's what you tripping about? Them thangs been in there forever."

"I guess the earring and lipstick too? Even though you clean yo' car out every week? You know what? I'm going to bed, I don't even care," she said before turning the light off and walking to the bedroom.

Once she got in the bed, everything hit her at once. Malachi, Brian, Nigel's cheating ass and her pregnancy. Her tears caught in her throat, and she felt exhausted by it all. The bed dipped, and she felt the heat from Nigel's body before he put his leg over hers.

"Look, lil' baby, that's probably Leaisha's earrings. You know Rod uses my truck sometimes. Come on, stop tripping, mane!"

"I don't know nothing! All I know is that now that I'm big and pregnant, you probably out there looking for someone else!" Her deepest fears slipped out unintentionally and released the torrent of tears. Her entire body shook with the pain from her heart.

Nigel pulled her close. "Come on now, Lissa. You ain't got to worry about that. I am not going nowhere, I promise you that. What you want me do?"

The warmth of his body and his words felt good, but she knew promises were made to be broken. The story of her life!

Nigel held her tightly until her body stopped shivering. "I just want you to love me."

Nigel wiped her face with his thumbs, seeming to study her. "You don't have to worry about that. I got you."

Kalissa smiled and snuggled closer to him but stopped short when she felt his hardness. "Uh-oh, naw, this ain't that type of forgiveness. Not tonight."

"Bring yo' ass here, lil' mama. I jus' wanna hold you." Nigel laughed.

***

Taj felt like turning around as soon as he saw Narrow Lane Road. He had this same feeling every time he had made this trip recently. He took a deep pull from his blunt and promised himself that this would be the last time.

"Fuck it!" Taj said to the interior of the vehicle.

When he pulled into the driveway, Taj sat there smoking with his eyes closed. Finally, he got out of his car.

Zandra came to the door with some boy shorts and a sports bra on and nothing else. Since he had given her the cold shoulder for almost two weeks, she made sure that she was alone when he came.

"Tee! I thought you weren't coming," she exclaimed excitedly as she hugged him tightly.

"I tole you I was. What up?" he said, smoothly pushing her away from him.

"Nothing, other than I missed you," Zandra moved in close again.

"Yeah, yeah. Anybody else here?" Tee asked, walking towards her bedroom.

"Nope, it's just us," she said as she followed him like a puppy.

Once they were in the room, Taj began taking his shirt off. He placed it carefully on the chair and unbuckled his jeans. Zandra came behind him, he could feel her bare titties on his back, and her hands reached down in his pants, coaxing his dick alive.

Taj popped out of his jeans and boxers quickly, as she slinked down to the floor on her knees. Taj closed his eyes as she inhaled his dick, her mouth warm and wet. All he could see were the times she was still acting pregnant: When she played sick so that he would stay with her, calling him in the middle of the night, wanting food and guilt tripping him about not wanting a baby she had already lost. Then he thought about when Desi died, how she still didn't care about him hurting, she just wanted 'pregnancy' attention. Taj began punishing her mouth, slamming her head against his groin and not letting go until after he skeeted in her mouth.

When he opened his eyes, she was still on her knees, looking at him with tears in her eyes.

"What the hell was that, Tee?" she said while wiping her mouth.

Taj ignored her as he turned and began to put his clothes back on.

"What the fuck you doing? We ain't through, we hadn't even made love yet," Zandra spat.

"We wasn't gonna make love anyway. We just been fucking, but I got something to do. So I'm leaving." Taj didn't even turn around.

He heard her sniffle. "Taj this is the third time we been together but we still haven't talked about what happened. I mean I told you that I was gonna tell you once everything settled down, but I didn't get a chance to. If Lissa hadn't pushed me down the stairs, I was going to tell you at dinner. I swear I was!" Zandra pleaded her case.

"Even if I wanted to believe that, which I don't, you forget that you kept pretending to be pregnant. As far as I know, you wasn't never pregnant! And you keep lying on Lissa, so that tells me you still lying about everythang."

Zandra's tears stopped and she narrowed her eyes. "You still believe that bitch over me. She's probably the one that put that in yo' head! If you never believed me, why you been coming over here 'fucking' wit' me, as you say? Acting like we back together?" Zandra stood with her hands on her hips, titties heaving and hanging out.

"You right 'bout that. I should have never come back ova here. But I ain't neva tell you we was getting back together. There jus' some things you can't come back from. You lied to me, Zan! Not just a lil' lie, a whoppa of one. Don't you understand that?" Taj's nostrils flared with his anger as he patted his pockets for his keys.

"I said I was gonna tell you! Just leave, Tee, and don't ever come back. I don't have to be treated like this. I can find me a real baller tomorrow! So take yo' ass on," she snapped, jerking her shirt back on.

Taj wanted to knock the shit out of her, but instead he snickered. "A real baller, huh? You know what? I wouldn't care if Lissa did push yo' trifling ass down them stairs. You deserve all the shit you get, hoe."

"Get out! I shoulda never even messed wit' you in the first place wit' yo' cheap ass! Get the fuck out!" Zandra screamed at his back as he walked to the door.

Chapter Fifteen

Zo hustled into his uncle's house, disappointed that he didn't smell any food. His aunt—Reesie—let him in with a smile and a hug.

"You know where he is. Out back smoking them doggone cigarettes," she laughed, pointing towards the patio.

Zo stepped on the patio, and saw his uncle sitting on the edge of his lawn chair. James never looked back at him, and Zo jumped when he spoke.

"What you got going on, Zo?" James barked.

"Oh hey, Unc'. I just wanted to ask you if I could get my own set and spot? That nigga Rollo is crazy! We barely got anything to sell and then he act like he don't want nobody asking him a question," Zo blurted out.

"Boy, that ain't Rollo fault! Things is slow right now for everybody. You don't have product, cuz I'm having a hard time getting it." James lit his cigarette after replying Zo.

"What's going on, Unc'? Somebody else getting yo' shit?" Zo pulled out his own smokes and tried to hide the way his hand shook as he lit it.

"See, this is why you ain't ready for yo' own shit! You don't even understand supply and demand. Whenever there is a huge demand, yo' supply will be less which raises yo' prices. My distributor not only raised his prices, but I think he's having problems getting product. He ain't said nothing, but I been around long enough to know how this works. You just sit tight." James looked at Zo. "What you doing wit' yo' money anyway? Every time I see you, it look like you have on the same clothes, driving the same raggedy ass car. When you gonna get you a car?"

"Ain't nothing wrong with that one. It drive just fine," Zo retorted.

"It ain't yo' car! That's Ureka car and when she get tired of you, then what you gonna do? That's yo' problem, you don't want to lissen. Every time I try to tell you something, you got something to say! What else you wanted?" James glowered at Zo.

"Unc' I just don't want to work wit' Rollo no more. That nigga want me in the trap all day, then act like a bitch if I invite a friend over." Zo saw James open his mouth, so he rushed on. "I ain't even talking about them being around the product. I jus' be trying to do a lil' something and this nigga tried to lay hands on me. I ain't gon' ever be able to have shit as long as I'm wit' him. Humph."

Zo leaned back in the chair and watched his uncle's reaction. James sat there silently for a few minutes, lost in his own thoughts.

"I can't just move you right now, Zo. But what I can do is give a lil' something on your own. I had put some extra away for Tee, so that he wouldn't feel the drought so bad. I can give some to you and see what you gonna do wit' it. This gonna be yo' money, but if you want more you gonna have to pay. This will be yo' test." James spoke almost to himself, but he was looking at his nephew.

"I can do it, Unc', I promise," Zo said with a big grin.

"I'm also trusting you not to mention this to Rollo. He might not think that it's right that I held back for Tee and not him. So, I want to see how you gonna pull this off."

"Mane, fuck what that nigga think. I'ma handle my shit, I promise you that," Zo said vehemently, rocking in his chair.

"If you fuck up, don't come back my way, you jus' gonna have to deal wit' whatever Rollo dish out to you. And I mean that. And don't tell Tee either, cuz he gonna know you cutting into his profit." James stood up, pulling a set of keys out of his pocket.

"Unc', you gotta stop worrying about what everybody think! You the man! They have to do whatever you tell them. They either gonna sink or swim about yo' word."

Listening to Zo use the wrong saying made James pause. He hoped that he wasn't making a mistake. The promise he made years ago to look after his brother and sister's kids was beginning to wear thin.

"A'ight, go back to yo' car until I call you back in here," James told Zo.

"My car? What? You don't trust me or something?" Zo looked at his uncle in disbelief.

"I don't trust no one. That's how I became the man, as you say, and how I'm going to stay the man. Go on now, it won't take me long," James chuckled.

Zo rose and pulled his pants up before dragging his feet to make it to the front door.

***

A week later, Kalissa's warning about Zo still resonated with Rollo. He wasn't surprised. He just wondered why she told him and what that nigga had done to her to make her feel that way. It crossed his mind to mention Zo to James since he was going for his re-up, but he hadn't made up his mind.

There was a feeling that he couldn't shake that something was going on with James. Not in a good way either. The last time he picked up his product, it was less than usual. Hence the reason he was going to see James again so soon.

Rollo liked the spread where James lived. It wasn't too far from the city, but it was country. Quiet without any close neighbors. Rollo had plans, and he wanted something similar in his future. That's why he had been increasing not only his re-up, but his prices to his customers.

James was lying across his sectional when he got there but, of course, they had to go outside. Dusk was falling and the crickets, frogs and whatever other creatures were out made themselves heard.

Instead of stopping on the patio, which was lit up by solar lights around the deck and stairs, they walked out to the little pond in his back yard.

"You see that big ass frog? That's a bullfrog," James said, pointing at the biggest frog Rollo had ever seen in life.

The frog jumped in the pond with a big splash. Rollo"s mind changed slightly about getting a similar spread if this was the wildlife it came with. He wasn't 'bout that life.

"Lissen, I know you didn't come all this way to see no frogs, so I'm jus' gonna keep it real wit' you. I wasn't able to get anymore product this time. I don't know what the hell is going on with my distributor. He raised his prices a while back. I negotiated with him to keep ours about the same and I thought we were fine. Which we were for a minute. Then he came with he was having 'issues' getting the product. Shid, I didn't even say anything at first, cuz I had some in reserve. But now?" James shrugged and looked at Rollo.

"Damn. I hate that, cuz we are dry, I mean, *dry*," Rollo looked back at the pond. "What do you think it is?"

James finally lit his cigarette, and didn't speak until after he blew a huge puff of smoke.

"This is just what I think, ain't nobody told me shit. And this stays right here at this pond. I believe, nah, I know he's been selling to some niggas in Mississippi, probably at a higher price. Even though our numbers have been good, damn good, I think he's getting some heat in Alabama. So he's laying low, right now. That's just what I think." James pulled on his Newport, before he continued. "I also think he's about to get out of the game."

"Word? Why if everything is going good?" Rollo asked, moving his feet around in the grass, clearly uncomfortable.

"Come on, mane, let's go to the patio," James laughed, noticing Rollo's discomfort. "I guess you don't like nature, huh?"

"Hell naw! I got enough of that shit in the Marines," Rollo laughed as he turned to walk to the patio.

"I'ma tell you what a wise man once told me. You get out when the going is good, not when something happens or when things get hot. If you wait until then, you'll get hemmed up." James continued his story once they sat down on the patio.

"Makes sense."

"Now I'm trying to find another distributor for just in case. I tried to ask Waski, but that nigga still mad about how shit went down in Tuskegee." James peered at Rollo.

Rollo looked at him but didn't say anything, he just nodded. When James didn't continue, Rollo tilted his head to the right and finally broke the silence.

"Mane, Tank dissed me and got exactly what he asked for. He killed his mans cuz he was on that bullshit. You know how it goes." Rollo never broke eye contact.

James looked down at his hands, nodding. Rollo stood, signaling his exit.

Speaking slowly before he stood, James said: "Ro, sometimes the best response is no response. I know you big on your respect, and I understand that, but killing is not always the answer. You can't solve everything wit' yo' piece."

"You right, but you also know how it goes. If I let a nigga diss me in front of my crew, what you think gonna happen?" Rollo's eyes glimmered in the night.

"Yeah, I do know how it goes. I also know that it eats at you, keeps you from sleeping at night, all those bodies on yo' brain." James' deep voice was low but resonated in the stillness of the night.

Rollo rubbed his chin. "Maybe if them niggas meant something to me or maybe if they wasn't no fools that wouldn't go after my family or yours, then I might lose some sleep. But them ordinary niggas? I sleep jus' fine." Rollo shrugged. "Jay, I have accepted all that comes wit' this life. Either you play the game or you get played by it. Ain't no in between. And me? I always play to win." Rollo splayed his hands out.

"You right, you shole right." James cleared his throat. "Hopefully, once this dry spell passes, we'll be back to regular business."

"I hope so, but I'll hold it down wit' my crew, they'll be straight. Just hit me up when the package is ready," Rollo said.

"One mo' thing before you go. How is Zo doing?" James asked.

Rollo paused and rubbed his index knuckle up the middle of his nose. "He a'ight. Still wet behind the ears and adjusting. But it ain't nothing I can't handle."

James nodded and after shaking hands, Rollo let himself out. Alone with only the frogs croaking and the crickets chirping, James regretted giving Zo anything. For as long as he knew him, James knew Rollo hadn't put hands on Zo for 'having fun'. Either Zo lied or did some foul shit. If anyone should have gotten the reserve, it was Rollo, who had always been loyal. Time would tell how much that mistake would cost him. He hoped Zo would keep his mouth shut, but deep in his heart James knew Zo was going to fuck up.

Chapter Sixteen

"Oh I know what I been meaning to tell you, but you run out that door so quick, I be forgetting," Rayven said to Kalissa, as she tried to run out of the door again.

"What's that?" Kalissa asked, half listening because she knew how Rayven liked to gossip.

"Gul, this fine man kept coming in here looking for you, but then we found out he was Brian's brother!" Rayven laughed. "Now why you didn't tell me that Brian had a bruh that looked like that?"

Shock waves shot through Kalissa.

"When? Yesterday?" Rayven had her full attention now.

"Umm, no it was last week. He came in here and sat at that table right by the door. Until Darius finally told him that you work during the day." Rayven smacked her lips. "He stopped coming then."

"Darius? How did Darius tell him anything? Wasn't he in the kitchen?" Kalissa tried to act nonchalant, but she was steaming inside. Big mouth Darius! That was probably who Brian's homeboy was.

"Nah, you know how after his shift Darius likes to sit at the bar, drink, talk shit and watch sports. I don't think that nut has a TV at home, the way he hangs around here." Rayven laughed at her own joke.

Kalissa didn't even crack a smile. "Yeah, he stopped by here the other morning. He just wanted to know if I knew anybody that had beef with Brian. But I didn't."

"Umm-hmm, that's what he asking all of us. You know, Brian didn't really talk to anybody but you when y'all was together. And him and Darius would cut up sometimes in the back. So, we all told him that we were shocked when it happened because he just seemed straight and kinda nerdy. Well, we didn't tell him that part," Rayven went on.

Kalissa heard her but wasn't really listening because all she could see was Brian holding his hand out, asking for help, then the light going out of his eyes. The memory was so sharp she had to close her eyes.

Rayven continued: "Gul, look at me going on and on. I know that hit you hard. I can tell sometimes when you be looking back in the kitchen where he used to be. I just be talking, don't pay me no attention."

Opening her eyes, Kalissa gave her co-worker a small smile. "I'm okay, it was just so unexpected, ya know? But anyway, girl, I've got to run. Hold down the fort."

"All right. You be careful driving home."

Kalissa waved and headed out the door. The first instinct was to call Nigel, but she thought better of it. This piece of news she would keep to herself because she did not want anyone else to get hurt. Enough damage had been done.

Once outside, she slowed down when she saw a car parked beside hers. It wasn't the same car Malachi had been in. When the person got out, she realized it was Fefe. Everybody wanted to come to her job with the bullshit!

"Hey! So, it is true. You are pregnant. Congratulations!" Fefe said loudly, as if they had been talking to each other all along.

"Thanks," was all Lissa said, shaking her keys.

"Since you won't accept my calls or answer my texts, I just wanted to come here to apologize." Fefe started off slow, then her pace picked up. "Lissa, you know if I thought you and Nigel were going to hit it off, I would have told you! And I promise you we had stopped fooling around by the time you met him. I just figured since he was in the streets you wouldn't have been interested. The next thing I know, y'all were together and I didn't know how to tell you!"

Kalissa was tired. Tired of the drama, the lies and secrets. She searched her friend's face for any insincerity but found none.

"Fefe, I just wished you had said something. If I had known, I would have never fooled wit' him! Then Zandra throwing it in my face like me and her did the same grimy shit!" Kalissa leaned against her car.

"Girl, the only reason Zan knew was because she had come over once unannounced and Nigel was there. But it was never anything like that. We were just kicking it, no relationship or nothing. I mean I'll be honest. I did feel some type of way seeing how he treated you, but that was just jealousy." Fefe looked down at the ground.

That was the Fefe Kalissa knew. Always honest even if it didn't make her look good. Even when all of her other so-called friends had dropped her when she got pregnant with Jamila, Fefe stuck with her. Fefe was the only person she told about Zandra's betrayal. The words Zandra slung at her about forgiving Terry but not her slapped her in the face. Nigel was forgiven, so why should she hold a grudge against Fefe?

"That's what I mean. I never want to make you feel that way about me. Things could be so different if you had just told me!" Kalissa stressed.

"I didn't want to hurt you. And if he makes you happy, you deserve it," Fefe said plainly.

Out of nowhere, Kalissa's tears fell down her face. It wasn't just her friend's kind words and heart, she also thought about all the things that could have been different. There wouldn't have been a club incident, Brian would still be alive, and there probably wouldn't have been any reason for everyone to be at her house the night Desi got killed. So many things wouldn't have happened.

"Aww, don't cry! Lissa, I swear, I'm not jealous anymore! I just want our friendship back." By this time, Fefe was crying too.

It felt as if a weight had been lifted off of her heart through her tears. Kalissa chuckled while she rummaged through her purse, looking for a tissue.

"Look at us! Out here in the parking lot of my job, crying! I guess this pregnancy has me all emotional," Kalissa said, pulling herself together.

"My grandma always said crying is good for your soul. So don't feel bad about it," Fefe said, accepting the tissue Lissa handed her.

"I guess. Your grandma had something to say about every-thing."

"And you know this, mane. Seriously though, can you forgive me?" Fefe looked down at Lissa earnestly.

"Girl, yeah, you know you're my Ace Boon Coon," Lissa smiled.

The women hugged tightly, rocking each other, not caring who saw them. When they broke apart, they laughed, all tension gone.

"Girl, you and Taj are going to drive me crazy! Y'all know I don't have any other friends," Kalissa stated honestly.

"Plenty of people want to know you. Yo' ass just don't trust nobody," Fefe was still wiping her face. "Taj is the reason I decided to try your job. If that nigga can forgive Zan, I just knew you could forgive me!"

Fefe's words stopped Lissa in her tracks. Cocking her head to the side, she frowned and drew her lips up to her nose. "What do you mean? I know you lying! Please tell me that Taj did not get back wit' that hoe!"

"Humph, according to Zan, they been 'talking'. But you know how she lies, so maybe not." Fefe looked at Lissa sheepishly. "She probably is lying, because me and her are supposed to be going out tonight. Maybe I shouldn't."

"Why not?"

"Cuz I was just going because I was bored. But since we have made up, I feel kinda funny going out with her. You know she almost destroyed not just our friendship, but you and Taj too. I don't know." Fefe looked as if she wanted Lissa to make the decision for her.

"Chile, go and have a good time. I mean, you'd already planned it. Just don't tell that heifer any of my business," Kalissa's hand went to her stomach.

"You know I don't play that shit. I ain't even telling her no more of my business." Fefe laughed, then turned serious. "I'm glad I came and I didn't realize how much I missed you until now."

"Aww, I missed you too. It was killing me to ignore yo' ass," Lissa laughed.

The women hugged again, before they parted. They never saw the car tucked in the dark corner where Malachi watched the entire scene.

C.D. Blue

Chapter Seventeen

Fefe waited in the car for Zandra to come. She had told her thirty minutes ago that she was on her way, and the heifer still wasn't ready! Fefe checked her mirror once again to make sure her make-up was straight.

Zandra finally walked out the door in a short red dress. It was low-cut but loose around her ass. Probably because she didn't have much of one.

"Girl, sorry about that. The first outfit I chose just didn't feel right. I had to sneak this one out of my momma's closet," Zandra laughed as she got in the car.

"I was about to leave yo' ass," Fefe threatened as she pulled off.

They got to the club, and Fefe hoped that Nigel would not show up with the same chick she had seen him with before. That would be all Zandra needed to try to hurt Lissa.

Inside the club the lights were dim, and it was crowded with the usual party folks in town. People were clustered up in their cliques, checking out everyone else that walked through.

"Y'all ladies shole looking good," the man at the door grinned at them.

"Good enough to get in free?" Zandra flirted back.

"Now baby, if this was that kinda place, you know I'd let you in with no problem, but—" the door man said.

"Whateva, nigga," Zandra replied, throwing her cover charge at him.

"Girl, let's sit at the bar, it look like a bunch of lame hoes that can't get nobody done took all the tables," Zandra said, as she passed a few tables.

"Bitch, I ain't fighting tonight, so you need to get off whateva you on," Fefe said to her once they sat at the almost empty bar.

"Fuck them hoes! They know I'm telling the truth. I came here to meet somebody and I ain't leaving until I do!" Zandra said, smiling at the bartender as she moved her shoulders to the beat of "Temperature" by Sean Paul.

"What? You just told me that you and Taj was getting back together? What happened to that?" Fefe asked.

"Humph, Taj on that stupid shit. So, while he getting himself together I'mma do me," Zandra rolled her eyes.

"All righty then," was Fefe's only response as she looked around to see who was there.

When the bartender set drinks in front of both of them, they looked at each other and raised their eyebrows.

"It's from the young man over there," he told them with a smirk.

"See, that didn't take long at all. Taj just don't know!" Zandra said excitedly.

"Girl, that's Boo Man, I don't know about you but don't nobody want his ass," Fefe shot back once she saw who the bartender was talking about.

Boo Man was about five foot seven and three hundred pounds. He hit on every female that passed by him.

"Aw shit! Now that nigga know betta. He ought to—uh-oh, look at this tall drink of water that just walked in!" Fefe nudged Zandra so hard her drink splashed on her.

A fine, tall, chocolate bald head dream had just walked in. He looked at her, smiled, with perfect white teeth. Fefe's panties got wet just from his smile.

"Hmm, and it looks as if he has his eyes on you. Let me move out of the way," Zandra muttered.

"Come to momma, baby," Fefe whispered as she sat straighter and adjusted her top. She pulled it down, making sure that her babies were at attention.

"Is anyone sitting here," the chocolate wet dream asked in Fefe's ear.

His voice was deep and melodic, Fefe was about to come just from the sound of it.

"Nope, not at all," Fefe squeaked out. She was embarrassed as soon as she heard her voice.

114

He sat down and the not only did he look good, but he also smelled divine! His cologne wafted up her nose, and she squirmed from the moistness of her panties.

"What kind of cologne is that you're wearing?" Fefe asked, ready to throw her mack on him.

"It's Givenchy, I forget the name. You must want to get some for your man?" he said while looking into her eyes.

"No, I don't have a man. It just smells so good I wanted to know," Fefe giggled.

"Oh, okay, in that case, I'm Malachi and you are?"

"Felicia."

"Nice to meet you, Felicia. What's wrong with the men in this city to let a beautiful woman like you stay single?"

Before Fefe could answer, she felt Zandra's hand swoop by her.

"Since Fefe has lost her manners, I'll introduce myself. I'm Zandra," Zan said, leaning over far enough to show her navel.

"Nice to meet you too," Malachi said with a smile.

"Like I was saying, Felicia, how is it possible for you to be single?" Malachi went right back to his conversation.

"Your guess is as good as mine." Fefe smiled, feeling on top of the world.

"Wait a minute! Before you get my homegirl's stats, what about you? It don't matter if she's single if you ain't." Zandra busted in loudly.

Heat flushed through Fefe's body as she turned to set Zandra straight. Her arm moved faster than her body, and her drink tumbled over on her! Malachi caught it, but he wasn't quick enough. The amber liquid splashed against her shirt.

"Damn!" Fefe cursed more at Zandra than the drink.

"Girl, you betta go to the bathroom and put some cold water on that before it stains," Zandra drawled slowly.

Fefe batted her eyes at Malachi. "Excuse me, I'll be right back."

"I'll be here waiting on you, beautiful," he said with a wink.

Fefe strutted to the bathroom, knowing that her ass had him captivated. She wanted to look back but didn't want to seem obvious. Humming when she entered the restroom, she decided to go ahead and pee, so that she would not have to leave this man's side the rest of the night. It finally seemed as if her luck was changing.

Fefe's shirt was a blue and white polka dot crossover shirt, and the brandy had landed right on one of the white polka dots. Running some cold water over a paper towel, she wiped it as well as she could, to no avail. With a shrug, she patted on some powder, freshened up her lipstick and smacked her lips. Satisfied with her looks, she stepped out.

An extra swish was in her hips when she walked back to the bar, but stopped short when she saw Zandra had slid over to her seat and was damn near in Malachi's lap. Before letting her anger get the best of her, she stood by an empty table to watch her so-called friend.

Zandra was laughing at something Malachi said while rubbing his arm. Then she whispered in his ear, and he pulled out his phone. Fefe watched as Zandra pecked at his phone with her thumb before handing it back to him.

It was more of a stomp that got her back to the bar. Zandra looked at her with a smile, but made no move to get back to her own stool.

"I was about to come get you, it took so long!" Zan said loudly with a giggle.

"I bet you were. You gonna get out of my seat?" Fefe said without cracking a smile.

"Oh shit! My bad. Let me move out of your way."

It hadn't escaped Fefe's attention that Zandra had hiked her skirt up and was sitting with her legs wide open while she was talking to Malachi.

Fefe rolled her eyes as she slid on the barstool. Malachi looked at her and smiled. The scene she had just witnessed watered down her excitement for him.

"You alright?" he asked.

"Yeah, I'm fine, so are you from here?" Fefe tried to shake her anger away.

"Originally, but I've been living in Mobile. I came home after my brother died," he answered, looking down.

"Oh! I'm sorry. I can't imagine how that feels," Fefe exclaimed.

"Yeah it's been rough, especially on my mom. So, I'm here to help her." Malachi looked at Fefe with sorrowful eyes.

The combination of his bald head, deep-set eyes and sexy lips made her melt. The earlier anger she felt for him and Zandra disappeared. At least for him, anyway. Zandra had hopped off to talk to some female, but kept her eyes on the two of them. Fefe noticed it, so she made sure that she touched Malachi's arms and thigh every chance she got.

"Can I call you sometimes?" he asked.

"Sure, that wouldn't be a problem," Fefe said, as she quoted her number to him. She didn't ask for his because she knew she would call too quickly, and she wanted him to call her.

Once that was accomplished, Fefe was ready to leave. As soon as Zandra walked back to her seat, Fefe stopped her.

"I'm ready to go," Fefe said, harsher than she meant to.

"What? Already?" Zandra exclaimed, glancing at Malachi.

"Yes, I am. You coming with me or not?" Fefe asked while pulling her purse onto her shoulder.

Half of Fefe expected Zandra to pull some hoe shit, like ask Malachi for a ride, but the other half hoped she wouldn't. No matter what she did, Fefe knew that she was through with Zandra. For good.

"Well, I guess. How else would I get home?" Zandra said, still looking at Malachi.

"Hey, it was nice meeting you ladies. Y'all be safe," Malachi said, standing up.

He gave both women a one arm hug, but Fefe swore that he held her a little bit longer than he did Zan, who stood there licking her lips and damn near undressing the man with her eyes.

"Come on, let's go!" Fefe almost yelled at her friend.

Zandra got in the car, mumbling, "I see why you ain't getting no dick."

"Everything isn't about dick, Zan." Fefe sighed, exasperated.

"That's why you don't get any," was Zan's reply.

The rest of the ride was in silence. Fefe was mad and determined that this was the last time she would hang out with hoeish ass Zan.

Chapter Eighteen

Rollo pulled up at Duck's house and blew the horn. Duck came out within a few minutes, cheesing as usual.

"What it do, mane?" Duck leaned into the car from the passenger side.

"Come on, ride wit' me. I need to check out some shit," Rollo responded, unlocking the doors.

Duck jumped in without any further questions. They rode in silence, both men bopping their heads to "Regulate" by Warren G.

"Mane, you always listening to this old shit!" Duck laughed, still bopping his head.

"Bruh, Warren G don't never get old," Rollo responded with an incredulous look.

"Whateva, nigga. Where we headed? Duck asked, knowing that conversation wasn't going anywhere.

"I wanna see how everybody else doing during this dry spell." Rollo tapped his fingers against the steering wheel.

They pulled into an apartment complex close to Alabama State's campus. A few of Taj's crew were hanging around a Nissan Maxima, keeping their eyes on one man with his head stuck inside an older Buick.

"For us to be so damn dry, they seem pretty damn busy," Duck mused, watching the action around him.

"Umm-hmm," was all Rollo said.

They left that spot and went to a few of Rod's spots. They was slinging like crazy. Duck sat with his eyebrows furrowed, and he kept glancing over at Rollo.

The final destination was off Fairview in one of their own slower spots. It seemed pretty quiet until they saw a car pulling off.

"Ain't that the nigga from 'Skegee? What the fuck is he doing?" Duck yelled.

"Bruh, calm down. We 'bout to see," Rollo said, gliding his car into the spot the other had just left.

Trev smiled once he realized who they were.

"What up, youngblood?" Rollo asked after letting his window down.

"Not much, mane. We pretty slow, I'm just doing a lil' something wit' the regulars," Trev smiled, showing his gold.

"Where you get them rocks from?"

"Zo gave them to me. He said he was able to get a lil' something since he the big man blood." Trev noticed the looks between Duck and Rollo. "I mean that's cool, ain't it? You knew about it, right?"

"Aye, you cool. As a matter of fact, you don't even have to tell Zo you saw me tonight. A'ight?"

Trev looked uncertain, but nodded. Duck leaned over the console and whispered in Rollo's ear. Rollo looked from Duck back to Trev before nodding.

"Get in, youngblood, let me holla at ya for a minute," Rollo said to Trev.

***

"Aye, mane, drop me off at Mia's," Duck said after they dropped Trev back off.

"You still fucking wit' that hoe?" Rollo looked at Duck in disbelief.

"Yeah, mane, but not like that. She just something to do now. That bitch showed me her true colors too many times. I just know that during these dry times, she'll feed a nigga and buy me something to drink."

"You should be saving yo' money instead of wasting it on these hoes. Then you wouldn't have to deal with a treacherous hoe like Mia. A bitch only got to show me once. Anything more than that, I swear I'd have to kill her ass."

"Shidd, I am saving. I don't want to use my savings when I can make that hoe spend. Don't worry, when I meet my queen, Mia ass better not even look my way." Duck nodded.

"I need you to ride wit' me one more place, then I'll take you over to that stankin' ass hoe," Rollo shook his head.

120

He didn't wait for a response from Duck before dialing someone on his phone.

"Where you at?" Rollo listened intently. "Shoot me the address, I'm headed yo' way."

A short time later, they pulled into an apartment complex parking lot. Duck recognized it as one of the better hoods, but it was still the hood.

"Do I need my burna?" Duck asked.

"Nah, we good. Nigel's woman lives here, and I think she has a kid, so leave yo' shit in the car." Rollo directed.

Nigel opened the door when they made it upstairs. The TV was blaring, toys were strewn around the floor, and the small apartment smelled of food and pressed hair.

"Hey lil' sis, this is Duck," Rollo said, addressing Kalissa who was sitting in the dining area while Leaisha twisted her hair.

"Dennis? Is that you?" Kalissa squealed.

"Lissa? Aw shit! I ain't seen you since school. Where the hell you been hiding?" Duck replied.

"Here and at work. What you been up to?"

"Just hanging out wit' this OG, that's 'bout it," Duck replied, smiling.

Kalissa introduced Leaisha to the men before they walked over to the living area.

"What's going on, mane? I tole you to come here cuz you sounded like you on some emergency shit," Rod said, looking at Rollo and Duck after they sat down.

"Ya know I need to talk business," Rollo said quietly, cocking his head to the side towards the women.

The men rose and went outside. Kalissa's eyes followed their movement. Nigel blew her a kiss to which she responded by sticking her tongue out.

"Lissa will probably have her ear to the window, trying to hear. Wit' her nosey ass," Nigel joked as soon as they made it downstairs.

Once they settled in Rod's car, Rollo wasted no time getting straight to the point.

"Mane, how y'all staying so busy in this drought? I'm riding around the city and looks like everyone shaking shit up, but me," Rollo complained.

Nigel and Rod looked at each other. Then Rod spoke, "Well I'ma tell you this just on the strength that I know I can trust you not to run and tell. We been getting some product from somewhere else. James ass been cutting us short for a while. That's when I knew if I wanted to make some real chedda, I'd have to find another way."

Rollo narrowed his eyes and nodded for Rod to continue.

"James gives us enough to live but he damn sho gonna make sure we can't make it like he making it. I saw that shit way before this 'dry period'. So one of my cousins down in Florida put me on to another source. I can get as much as I can afford to pay for." Rod smiled, his one gold sparkling in the darkness.

"Damn, that's what's up. What about the other homies? You put them on too?"

"Who? Taj? Hell naw. They cool and all but that's James fam, you know he would tell." Rod shook his head as he spoke.

"Hmm, you sho right. And James gonna make sure he take care of his fam," Rollo was nodding as if he was listening to music.

Rollo's head stopped bopping as soon as he began speaking: "Check this out, mane. Put me on and I'll spot you a key for the favor. Cuz we hurting right now."

"Mane, you ain't got to spot me shit! Just make sure yo' money right and we keep this in this car. Once James get straight again, I still want to fuck wit' him too. I'm trying to blow the fuck up." Rod looked between Duck and Rollo.

"No worries, I ain't telling shit." Rollo rotated his neck, cracking it. "I got a bone to pick wit' Jay ass, but I'ma hit you later and get wit' you on how much I need."

"Bet, I'll need to know by the next day or two cuz I got a shipment to pick up soon," Rod said, smiling.

"Nigga I'm straight. Ion know what you been picking up yo' shit up in, but you might need a truck this time around," Rollo said before getting out the car. "Lemme go tell lil' sis bye before she give me hell the next time I go in Applebee's."

"And you know her ass will. You won't get shit free!" Nigel laughed.

Kalissa and Leaisha were in same spot. Lissa stood when the men walked in, looking at them suspiciously.

"A'ight, lil' sis, thank you for welcoming us in yo' home," Rollo said smoothly.

"Are y'all brothers?" Lissa asked, looking from him to Duck.

Duck covered his mouth with his fist as he laughed. "Damn, how you know?"

Lissa smiled slyly. "I could just tell. Y'all be safe out there."

"Lil' sis, you must be psychic or something. It's niggas hang wit' us every day and don't know we related. How the hell you figured that out in less than ten minutes?" Rollo asked.

"Most people look at shades, I look at features. Plus, I can read folks, easily," Lissa sassed back. "Well, almost everyone." She glanced at Nigel and smiled.

Everybody laughed except Nigel, as Rollo and Duck left out.

C.D. Blue

Chapter Nineteen

The sun shined brightly through Fefe's curtains. Her movements reflected how she felt, slow. Usually, she was up, dressed and ready to go every morning before eight, whether she had to work or not. The past month had taken its toll on her. When she met Malachi, she felt a connection like never before, so she went back to the way she was raised. Take it slow, get to know a person and let the feeling flow naturally. The only time she hadn't done that was with Nigel. That had been pure lust.

Fefe had watched her friends and cousins jump into bed with a man, and—if it didn't work—repeat the process until it did. When she met Nigel, she had decided to try their way and ended up catching feelings, but only being a booty call. Malachi had seemed too special to ruin her chances.

It seemed to be working at first. They talked on the phone, and even had lunch a few times. Nothing more. At times he seemed into her and other times he seemed distracted; she put it off as his obsession with his brother's death. He didn't talk about it much, but she knew that it was heavy on his mind. Every time he brought it up, she would change the subject to get his mind off of it.

Everything changed when Zandra called her a few days ago to tell her that she was going out with Malachi! That bitch had been talking to him the entire time behind her back. Fefe could tell that it wasn't their first date, just the first one Zandra had decided to share.

When she didn't hear from him that night or the next day, not only did she know it was true, but she knew they were fucking. Fefe was done with both of them.

With a slight shake of her head, she tried to put her on her make-up before Lissa came to pick her up. Fefe didn't even know where they were going, just that Lissa told her to be ready. As much as she didn't want to get of bed, she knew she needed to get out of the house before she lost her mind.

Twenty minutes later, she heard the knock on her door. Forcing a fake smile, she answered.

"Guhl, look at you! You look ready to pop!" Fefe smiled as she took in Lissa's big belly.

"I know, this baby is like a basketball. It doesn't help that he's so low and he keeps tapping on my thighs." Lissa smiled. "You ready?"

"Yeah, let me get my purse. Where are we going anyway?" Fefe asked, as she walked through her apartment, making sure all the lights were off.

"I wanna show you something. Just come on," Lissa laughed.

"Okay, I'm coming," Fefe murmured, thrown off a bit by Lissa's carefree manner.

They rode for about ten minutes, listening to "We Belong Together" by Mariah Carey, on repeat the entire way. Lissa pulled into the driveway of an unfamiliar white house.

"Who lives here?" Fefe asked.

"Come on, you'll see," Lissa said, unstrapping her seat belt.

When they got to the door, Lissa put a key in the door and opened it.

"Voila!" Lissa yelled with a little twirl.

"Bitch, I know you lying? This is your place?" Fefe yelled, looking around.

The front room had furniture Fefe had never seen but when they walked to the den, there was Lissa's sofa set from her apartment.

"Yep, Nigel surprised me with it. Gurl, I'm out the damn hood. At last!" Lissa finally answered ecstatically.

"Gurl, damn!" Fefe grabbed Kalissa's arms, and they did a dance.

"Is Nigel here?" Fefe stopped and whispered.

"Nah, girl, he's at work."

Fefe's eyes grew big and she covered her laugh with her hand. "Work? As in, a job? What the hell have you done with the Nigel everybody knows?"

Kalissa laughed. "Yes. As in, a job. I got tired of worrying about his ass getting hurt or killed in the streets. Not to mention, I was tired of calling the hospitals and jails every time he was late coming home. So I told him he needed a job."

Fefe sat on the sofa and processed what she heard. She was happy for her friend, but it also made her sad about her own sorry situation. Trying to muster a smile, tears fell from out of nowhere.

"Fefe! What's wrong?" Lissa sat beside her and put her arm around Fefe.

"I'm sorry, I'm happy for you, Lissa, I swear I am. I just know that I can't ever seem to catch a man's attention for real. Not one who wants to do all of this for me." Fefe waved one hand around the den.

"Aww, Fefe, that's not true! I thought you had met someone," Lissa cried out, still rubbing Fefe's back.

"I thought I did too. But that night I met him, Zan pulled one of her hoe numbers and beat me out, I guess. I was trying to do things the right way, but that stanking ass hoe told me a few days ago that she was going out with him. So, he had been talking to both of us at the same time! I thought for sure he was the one for me." Fefe was in a full sob.

"Zan? I thought you told me she was back with Tee?" Lissa asked.

"No. Obviously, that was one of her lies. I think they were talking, but Tee don't want her funky ass. And I don't blame him!" Fefe let her anger out.

"Oh, Fe, I'm so sorry. I hate this happened to you."

"I'm done, I mean completely done with that hoe this time. She knew I was feeling him and she still went after him. I know how she is, but once again I followed them damn feelings. I thought Malachi was being sincere and was the one for me. The whole time he had been fucking her!" Fefe's voice grew louder with each word.

The rubbing abruptly stopped.

"Who? What did you say his name was?" Lissa whispered.

"Malachi. Remember I told you I met him that night after you and I made up. I probably didn't tell you his name, because I wanted to be sure before I started giving him props and all. That was the only thing wit' sense that I did do." Fefe pulled her shirt up and wiped her face.

She turned to Lissa who sat there as if she was in a trance, her eyes locked on the black television screen.

"Lissa? Do you know him or something?" Fefe prepared herself to hear the worst.

Kalissa seemed to snap out of it. "Me? No, I don't know anyone with that name. I was just thinking about how lowdown Zandra is for pulling that same shit! This time on you. It don't make no damn sense."

"What you say? But that's my fault. I knew that bitch wasn't no good and kept hanging wit' her anyway. That bitch was listening to me talk about him and was fucking him the entire time!"

"Wait! How you know they been fucking?" Lissa gave a small laugh. "And you know how Zandra is, she might be lying about the date." Lissa tried to make Fefe feel better.

"Nah, because I started thinking about the times I wouldn't hear from him, I wouldn't hear from her ass either. She knew what she was doing. The only reason she probably told me about this date is because she found out he was talking to me. Bitch!" Fefe spat.

Kalissa hated to see her friend unhappy, especially when she was on cloud nine. However, after hearing who she was talking about, she was glad that Zandra was the hoe she was.

"You probably right. Fefe, you just got to stop giving your all so quick. That nigga probably would have ended up being the worst thing to happen to you. Especially if he chose Zan over you. And wasn't you with Zan that night?" Lissa looked perplexed.

"Yeah, that's when I saw that hoe in action." Fefe's tears had subsided, but she still sniffled.

"Well, you know Zandra ain't shit, but he ain't either. He saw y'all together, so he knew y'all were friends. If his intentions were good, he wouldn't have kept talking to her," Kalissa said slowly.

Fefe narrowed her eyes as she looked at her friend. "You know, you're right. I hadn't even looked at it from that angle. I was so mad at Zan." Fefe stood. "It probably is a blessing. Let Zandra's ass listen to him go on and on about his dead brother." She covered her mouth. "Lawd, that sounded so wrong. I didn't mean it like it sounded."

Fefe looked back at Lissa who was once again staring at the television that was not on.

"Lissa? You okay?" Fefe asked.

Kalissa gave a little laugh. "Yeah, I was just thinking. You know I could have forgiven Zan years ago, but I knew that if I did, she would have done it again. You just proved me right. She was always asking how could I forgive Terry and not her, but we were friends! Men may come and go, but friends supposed to last forever."

"Hmm, that's true. I hadn't thought about it like that. Come on! Enough of my sob story. I'm really happy for you, Lissa. You gonna show me the rest of the house? I wanna see little princess Jamila's room. Get up, girl!"

With both hands behind her, Kalissa pushed herself up with a grunt.

"Now you see what us big folks have to go through! I still can't believe Nigel done got a job and moved you out the hood!" Fefe laughed.

"Humph, he just don't know it, but he's going to marry me next. We need to be respectable." Kalissa gave a small smile.

"Gurl, if you get that man to marry you, I need yo'mutherfuckin' playbook! Shid, I'm meeting men and can't even get to third base!"

Fefe was so busy laughing at her own jokes, she never noticed the look of worry that crossed Kalissa's face.

C.D. Blue

Chapter Twenty

Zandra laid back in the huge king-sized bed, satisfied. Malachi was looking at his phone, while she watched him. Not only was he fine, but he had money. His bedroom was huge! There was a California King bed along with a recliner, dresser, nightstands, and plenty of floor space left. Malachi was renting an older home off Perry St. in the old money part of town. His house had four bedrooms, a living room, den and a newly remodeled kitchen. Zandra knew that Fefe had her eyes on him first, but she wasn't letting this one go. He was a true baller.

"What you smiling about over there?" Malachi pulled her close to his body.

"How glad I am I met you. You came at the perfect time," Zandra smiled, snuggling close.

"Oh yeah? I'm just surprised you are single. I mean you're beautiful, smart and got a lot going for yourself. Usually, women like you are tied up wit' somebody."

Zandra smiled so hard her cheeks hurt. This was what she needed. Taj had never said those things to her.

"Oh my gosh! You are truly special. My last boyfriend never said anything so nice to me. It feels good to be appreciated for who I really am." Zandra gushed.

"That nigga must have been blind and dumb. What happened to him? I'm not going to have to beat nobody ass, am I?" Malachi chuckled.

"We broke up for good. He was too busy trying to please his 'best friend' instead of me. Never had time for me, but whenever she called, he had to run," Zandra spat bitterly.

"Hmm, so his best friend is a woman? That usually doesn't work out too well. Were they more than friends?" Malachi had gone back to looking at his phone while he talked.

"Plttt, he said they weren't and even after she got a man, he still be running up behind her. Like a damn fool." All of Zandra's anger came out as she talked about it.

"I'm surprised her man doesn't put an end to their friendship," Malachi half listened as he sent another text to Fefe. She hadn't responded to his calls or texts lately.

"Humph, Lissa has everyone that knows her fooled. She puts on this Ms. Goody-two-shoes act that all men seem to fall for. They can't seem to see that she's all for herself."

Zandra felt Malachi's thigh, which was trapped between her legs, stiffen.

"You alright, babe?" she asked with concern.

"Yeah, just a lil' cramp," Malachi placed his phone on the nightstand. "What did you say her name is?"

"Kalissa, we just call her Lissa. Well, I don't call her shit. That bitch pushed me down the stairs, and he believed her instead of me! That's why I broke up wit' his ass! I got tired of playing second to his so-called best friend."

"I'm glad you did, sweetie. You don't have to worry about that with me. It's just me and you and nobody comes before you," Malachi said smoothly.

Turning towards her, he kissed her while rubbing his hands down her body, coming back up to tweak her nipples.

"I think you are just who I've been looking for," he whispered seductively in her ear.

***

Instead of confronting James with what he knew, Rollo had been keeping his eyes on all the crews during the so-called drought. It was still the same. Taj was still moving product, and Trev was still slinging shit for Zo. Rollo had also found out that Zo had added some country ass niggas that called themselves a gang to his set. If Rod hadn't included Rollo in his little secret, his men would have been starving for a month. Or more. Rollo only included the homies that had been with him the longest, the ones he felt he could trust more than the others. That kept Zo out of the loop.

James had called for him to re-up finally, and Rollo knew he had an important decision to make. Thinking about James cutting him out but keeping his blood afloat made him remember what his mom had told years ago. When his mom found out that he was working for James when he got back from the military, she told him one thing before she put him out of her house:

"Work with him all you want, but don't never trust that nigga. He'll never let you get as big as him. That nigga will feed you to the wolves and act like he's helping yo' ass."

At the time, he just thought his momma was being overly cautious and was still mad that James was out doing his thang while her husband was locked up.

Rollo's dad had been in prison since he was twelve. He got caught with a shipment of drugs that he was picking up for James. All Rollo remembered was, life changed drastically after that. His mom, Elaine, was angry for many years after their dad left. Rollo became mad at her because she took him and his brothers to see his dad twice and never went back. She told them they could go see him once they were old enough to go alone. The other thing that bothered Rollo was him and his brothers were used to James coming around. His mom stopped that too. She told James not to come back around. Her exact words were, "Don't bring yo' black dusty ass around me never again."

What angered Rollo even more was how his dad was never upset with his mother, he always took up for her when he talked to his sons on the phone. Always told them to listen to her, do what she says, and told Rollo to always make sure he looked after his younger brothers. That's around the time Rollo started showing his ass. In school and around town. Elaine put her foot on his neck so hard, Rollo still felt it at times.

It wasn't until he was grown that Elaine explained why she stopped taking them to see their dad. Rollo didn't agree, but he understood her side of the story. The last time he went to see his dad was right before he left to go to the Marines. That's when he learned the whole story. Elaine's anger was not only justified, but Rollo decided he was done with his old man as well.

The closer he got to Hope Hull, the quieter it became. The noise of the city was only a few miles behind him, but it was as if he had driven to another state. James made sure he was far away from the griminess of the city, even though it was his dirt. Rollo hadn't driven his Impala, it brought too much attention. Instead, he was in a 2003 Buick LeSabre. Bigger trunk space, less fanfare.

Rollo stopped at James' home, once again marveling at how nice it was. It made him think about the little two-bedroom box in Mobile Heights he and his three brothers lived in when he was younger. That was the house his father had left them in.

With a grimace he straightened his face and thoughts before rolling his car up to the open garage. As soon as he pulled in, the loud sound of the wheels on the garage door started, closing him in. James stood at the entrance to the house.

James began, while wiping sweat off his face with a towel: "Hey! That was perfect timing, I just put yo' shit in here. The Big Man had me run through some hoops for this! He made the pick-up hard as hell! Damn near had to get to the moon and back. I'm getting too old for this shit."

"Maybe it's time to retire," Rollo joked.

"Shidd, I'm thinking about it. Just waiting on my nephews to get their shit together to run it. And not run it to the ground." James laughed.

Rollo took a step back, stung by this revelation.

"Yo' nephews? That's yo' plan for the future?" Rollo asked evenly.

"Well, yeah. You know they family, got to keep it in the family." James looked at Rollo strangely.

"You talm 'bout that fucked up nephew you put wit' me and the schoolboy? Them nephews?"

"That's why I said I got to give them time. I know Zo seems a lil' fucked up, but Taj will definitely be straight before him," James answered slowly while looking at Rollo questionably.

Rollo rolled his shoulders a few times, almost like a dance move, before straightening his posture. "Speaking of them, you wanna tell me why you was breaking them off during this dry period but leaving the rest of us to starve?"

"Hold up, now. First, I don't like yo' tone, nor do I have to explain a damn thing to you. If and I say *if* I had a few extras that I threw their way, it's 'cause they family. Not only that, they ain't been in the game as long as you and Rod. Now if y'all didn't have no money put away, that's on you. Not me." James had drawn up to his full height, and he gave Rollo the business.

Rollo stared back at him, not bucking under pressure. He kept his mouth closed, because he knew James wasn't through.

"And if this attitude is because I said I'll turn it over to them when I retire, mane, what you expect me to do? I'm the only family they got that can give them something. You know how it works. I told yo' dad I'd always look out for you and I will. But, I never promised you my place at the table. Never." James had softened his tone somewhat.

"And I never said I wanted it! Jay, you think I want to deal wit' all the shit you do? Playing nice with twelve, trusting niggas to handle my shit? That ain't me. What you see is what you get wit' me. Nah, but think of the other ones that have been there in da mud, cleaning up yo' shit! Jojo, Rod, hell, even Duck! What about them? How you think they gonna feel about being under niggas that need to be spoon fed?" Rollo threw his hands down in frustration.

"Y'all with have to deal wit' it, when that time comes. It's like any other job, ain't nothing guaranteed! Look, I told yo' dad that I would make sure you and yo' brothers were straight, and that's what I did. I have kept my promise." James raised his eyebrows as he looked at Rollo.

"This ain't 'bout my pops or no promises. This is about standing on principles! All y'all ole schools came up out of the dirt. Wasn't nobody handing out favors because of no bloodline." Rollo argued.

"That's true. But when I got to the top, I promised that mine wouldn't have to go through and do all that I did to make it. And once again I'm keeping my promise." James took a deep breath, making a face as if he was explaining something to a child.

Rollo's demeanor changed. He smirked. "Yeah, well, maybe you need to remember how you got to the top. This ain't no Fortune five hunnid company and yo' hands ain't clean."

With narrowed eyes James looked at Rollo for a few minutes before he spoke evenly. "In this line of work ain't nobody hands clean. Period. The work all y'all put in, you got paid for. Very well, as a matter of fact. But like I said, it don't guarantee no spot. As long as I've held up my promise to your dad, I'm good. My word is my bond."

"Nah, it don't guarantee no spot, but it ought to count for something. And you told my pops you would look out for us. That didn't necessarily mean put us on game. Seems to me you shoulda been trying to keep us out of the streets. Instead, I been in the trenches. And if you was going to elevate another nigga that been in the trenches wit' me, we wouldn't be having this conversation." The vein in Rollo's forehead stood out as he glared at James.

James paced as much as he could in the garage. His face glistened with sweat as he grabbed another small towel off a rack to wipe it.

"We shouldn't be having this conversation now. I ain't going nowhere anytime soon, but when I do give it up, them boys will be ready. As for you, the streets was yo' choice. I didn't hold a gun to yo' head." James spat, his anger coming out.

Rollo leaned against his car, nodding with his arms crossed. He didn't say a word he just watched James.

James threw his hands out in front of him. "You ain't got to say nothing, my mind's made up. When I'm ready to leave out, my nephews—my blood—will take my place. I'm building a legacy, mane."

James leaned back on the deep freezer that sat against the wall, his eyes never leaving Rollo's face.

Rollo dropped his head and chuckled, showing his deep dimples. He looked up and made a sweeping motion with his arms.

"Legacy? You calling the dope game a legacy? Nah, Jay, you know as well as I do these streets are about the survival of the strongest. Eat or be eaten alive. Yo' nephews ain't killed nothing but a few roaches. You want to have a legacy, let them run a few of yo' businesses."

James stood up straight. "This is my legacy. I run this mutha-fuckin' town. I might have come up from nothing, but this shit is in my blood and this town is going to stay in my family. I don't know what else to tell you."

"Mane, you ain't got to tell me shit. You said it all, right there. You can give all that shit to yo' boys. I'll make it on my own, cuz this shit is in my blood too." Rollo jangled his keys as he took the short steps back to his car.

James rotated his neck, cracking it. "So, you just gonna walk away? It ain't gonna be easy being on yo' own. Like I said, the Gump especially belongs to me. Mane, don't let yo' feelings make yo' pockets empty."

"This ain't personal, it's all bizness, I ain't mad at cha but I'm done. I'll stay out yo' way and as long as you stay out of mine, yo' dirt will stay six feet under. Ya' feel me?" Rollo didn't wait for an answer. Throwing up the peace sign, he got in his car and cranked it up.

James stood there for a few minutes, looking at him thought-fully, before he pushed the lever to let the garage door up.

Chapter Twenty-One

One Year Later

Taj and Cet rode down the Boulevard after setting their stash up at Kabir's store. Since Rollo had left James, they had been getting a bigger supply of pills.

"Mane, your uncle set us straight this time. I still can't believe Rollo left him. He had been with James for years!" Cet exclaimed.

"Lean Wit It, Rock Wit It"—by Dem Franchize Boyz—blared from Taj's woofers in his trunk. The entire car shook from the bass.

"I know, that shocked the hell out of me too. For real tho, I think Unc' was shocked the most," Taj agreed.

The light at Court Street stopped them and as they sat there, a maroon Pontiac G6 pulled up beside them. It was Zo and a light-skinned guy who looked vaguely familiar to Taj. Zo looked over at them and sneered.

"That nigga right there! At least his ass finally got a car, but I bet he still staying wit' Ureka in the damn projects," Cet said, while glaring back at Zo.

"Mane, you know it! And she still riding in that beat up ass Altima. That nigga won't do right to save his life. That's why I was surprised when Unc' gave him his own set." Taj shook his head, laughing while pulling off.

"Me too, and he is fucking up in 'Skegee! The easiest damn place to make some dough. And he still can't beat Rollo! I don't know who that nigga dealing wit' now, but did you see his new whip? That mug is clean as hell!" Cet bent over with laughter. "All his crew stayed wit' him, they didn't want to fuck wit' Zo at all."

"Unc' is still mad as hell too cuz Rollo won't tell him who he getting his dope from. I can't believe that somebody has the nerve to serve in Uncle's territory. That's some brave shit." Taj mused.

"Mane, word on the street is that Rollo left unc' cuz Unc' was fronting Zo some shit on the side and left Rollo out to dry." Cet half turned in his seat, looking at Taj.

"Ion know nothing about that. Unc' just told me they decided to go their separate ways." Taj's eyes never left the road.

"Jus' between you and me, I kinda believe it. Cuz how else Zo already had some niggas riding wit' him?"

"I don't know who them niggas is, but they wit' his ass, strong," Taj said.

"I see that. He rolling wit' them Blood niggas, half of them from Lowndes County. But Rollo's crew rode wit' him just on the strength of him. Them guys ain't gonna do that for Zo. Matter of fact, the nigga we just saw riding wit' him is that Lil Red dude brother. You remember him?" Cet was eating some barbeque pork skins as he talked.

"Yep, you told me somebody killed him." Taj kept his eyes on the road as he turned on Air Base Blvd, headed to Gibbs Village.

"Umm-hmm, they call him Gedo, or some shit like that. I think his ass wit' Zo because he think somebody in Rollo's camp killed his brother. He damn shole ain't loyal to Zo." Cet reported the news like he was a newscaster. "That gang of his ain't never slang no dope. Them niggas be hitting licks. Zo betta watch his back. They'll rob his ass too."

"That ain't my problem," Taj said as he pulled into Gibbs Village.

"Why we here, mane?" Cet asked, easing his piece out.

"Naw, mane, ain't nothing like that. I just need to drop something off. Slow yo' ass down, I'll be right back." Taj laughed as he got out of the car.

Taj met a familiar looking woman at her door. Cet saw him pull a roll out of his pocket and hand it to her. She smiled and gave Taj a hug and kiss before he hustled back to his ride.

Taj slid back into the driver's seat without saying a word. Cet looked at him and grinned.

"Naw, mane, who was that? I saw you give her all yo' money. You been holding back on yo' boy?" Cet grinned.

"You know her! That's Rayven, she work wit' Lissa. We been kicking it a lil' bit," Taj said slyly with a smile.

"All that dough you just gave her? Y'all doing more than just a lil' bit," Cet laughed, punching Taj in the arm.

"Naw, mane, it ain't serious like that! I just gave her some ends to get her something to wear to Lissa's wedding. You going?" Taj looked over his sunglasses at Cet.

"Hell yeah! I mean I wasn't expecting that shit, but I'm here for it. I knew she was through when he moved her out the hood. Cuz you know that's all Lissa wanted." Cet shook his head.

"Come on now, it's more than that. She is into Nigel, like for real for real! She has had his baby, moved out of her own place and now she gonna marry him. That's something serious there. This ain't jus' bout her moving out the hood. She is in love." Taj sighed heavily. "And he loves her too. Shid, that nigga got out the game for Lissa and got a job."

"See, shit like that, y'all niggas can have. Ain't no bitch gonna take me away from my money. Hell naw!" Cet slammed his hand on the dashboard, and was shaking his head.

"You know how Lissa is. I think it was worrying about something happening to him. She ain't never liked no street niggas anyway. But after Desi got killed, she was worse. According to Fefe, she was driving herself crazy with worry." Taj rubbed his chin, still keeping his eyes on the road.

"Mane, Lissa don't look like she worry about nothing. It's hard to believe she'd be willing to give up certain things Nigel could do just to not have to worry about his ass." Cet was still shaking his head.

"That's how she look, but that ain't how she is. I just hope that nigga know what he got," Taj said with a sad smile.

***

"Stay in the present. Each step forward should be for your future. Leave the past where it belongs, behind you. You can't

change it, so dwelling on it will only leave you with regrets. That emotion can only hinder you from reaching your full potential."

That voice brought Kalissa out of her slumber. The more those visions came to her, the less she believed it was grandmother. They stayed with her so long she began to question whether or not she was losing her mind.

Shaking her head, she sat on the side of her bed. The house was quiet. Her children were at her sister's house, and Nigel was with Rod. Kalissa was definitely in the present. It was her wedding day, and nothing would stop her walking down the aisle. Not the past or future.

With a gleeful hop she skipped to her closet, checking to make sure her dress was still there. It was. This was her last day being a Garrett; she would soon be a Willis. A wife. Not a girlfriend or a baby momma, but a wife. They were going to be respectable. Nobody in her family would be able to look down on her because not only did she have two kids without a ring, they had different daddies. A big no-no for her folks.

Kalissa grinned as she thought about how it all unfolded.

They had been in their new home for two months when she brought up marriage.

"You know I'm not planning on living in sin for a long time," *she said to Nigel as she greased his scalp.*

He was sitting on the floor in between her legs but turned to look at her.

"Damn, Lissa, we just got into a house. Now you want to get married? Shid, you ain't never satisfied," *he grumbled.*

"I damn shole ain't going to be satisfied with shacking up. But anyway, I'm not talking about right now, I'm just letting you know for future reference." *Lissa smacked her lips, leaning back because the weight of her pregnancy was killing her back.*

"Humph, then if we get married, it will be something else," *Nigel muttered, turning back to the television.*

"Probably so, but you ought to be used to me by now," *she smiled, leaning forward to kiss him behind his ear.*

142

Justin, who was the spitting image of his daddy, was six months old when Nigel finally proposed.

Kalissa didn't want a wedding; for one, there wasn't enough time, and the other thing was that no matter what her friends saw on the outside, they had many struggles. Nigel wasn't that great about paying bills, Lissa had to damn near bust him upside his head to get him to do right. And of course, his job didn't pay as much as his last career. Which is why she worked almost right up to having Justin.

It wasn't that he didn't make the money, Nigel worked doubles at least twice a week. He just didn't know how to spend with just a paycheck. He made up for it with the children. Nigel treated Jamila as if she was his, which was good because Terry had gone ghost. Other than the child support that came like clockwork monthly. Justin would choose his daddy before he came to her. Nigel got up throughout the night for feedings, changed diapers, and was both kids' playmate.

Pushing those thoughts aside, she focused on what needed to be done. Her hair appointment was the first priority, then she would head to her sister's to get dressed and make sure the kids were straight.

A dark cloud hung over her head. Her mother was not attending her wedding. With the hard time that she gave Kalissa about being a single mom, Kalissa thought she would have been the happiest about her upcoming nuptials. But no, of course anything Lissa did was not good enough. Her mom wouldn't come to a ceremony that would only leave Lissa a widow or a prison wife since she wanted to be with a street nigga. These were the words from her mother that almost broke Lissa down.

Once again her father came to the rescue. He was happy, not ecstatic, but happy. Her dad was the one who convinced Lissa to get married in a church, instead of the courthouse. The older she got, the more she appreciated the man who raised her. It was time to stop looking for an approval that she would never get from her mother.

"There's no time to waste on thinking about this stuff either," Lissa whispered.

After a quick shower and throwing on some jeans and a button-down shirt, she could not risk messing up her hair or make-up, she rushed out the door.

Her stylist, DeShawn, was waiting for her. DeShawn was a tall, buff, bald headed good-looking chocolate gay man. Women swooned over him all the time, to his dismay and their disappointment. Kalissa loved him. She had met him while washing clothes in the laundromat attached to his shop. Lissa had swooned too, at first, until after her first appointment and she realized he was not into her or any other woman for that matter. They hit it off from the start and never looked back.

Four hours later, Kalissa walked out of his shop a glamorous queen. Her outfit felt beneath her all of a sudden. DeShawn had pulled her hair into a curly up-do and beat her face to perfection. She looked good, and her straight posture and runway walk told the story.

It was verified when her sister opened her door. "Oh my God! Gurl, look at you! I forget sometimes just how gorgeous you are, especially since you always downplay yo' looks. Jamila, come look at your momma!" Mahali screeched.

"Ohh Momma, you look so pretty!" Jamila squealed as she hugged Kalissa around her legs. Even Justin looked at her with interest.

"That man did the damn thang on your hair and face," Mahali murmured, walking around Lissa, inspecting her.

The next few hours went by in a blur, everybody got dressed, Fefe came over to help. Finally, her dad showed up to take her to the church.

A hush fell over the living room when Kalissa walked in from the back. Her wedding dress was simple but pretty. It was an off-white sleeveless fitted gown which flared at the bottom, and had a lace sequined overlay. Pearl earrings and a necklace completed her ensemble. Her shoes, while hidden by the dress, were silver open-toed six-inch sandals.

The ride was quiet mostly except her nerves seemed to jangle in her ear. Was she ready to settle down? In her heart she knew that Nigel was all she wanted, but her head whispered things that she didn't want to think about. Like how she really didn't trust him, how he still messed up money on stupidity, and how she honestly didn't trust his ass.

Her heart shot all those rational thoughts down when she got to the church and saw his truck in the parking lot. *He asked me because I'm the one he wanted for his wife, nobody else.* That ugly, arrogant pride took the front seat to all logic.

"You ready?" her dad asked. Kalissa nodded.

"Just remember you guys have to talk to each other no matter what the problems are," Henry gave his advice before opening his door.

There weren't any decorations, because this was supposed to be a small family affair. Kalissa was shocked when she and her dad stood in the doorway of the church. She saw, Taj, Cet, Rollo, Uncle James, her grandma, her aunt and even Duke. She stopped looking when Nigel caught her eye.

He and Rod stood on one side of the pulpit, while Mahali was on the other side. Nigel looked so good! With his hair growing out, he had a crisp cut and a wicked lineup. His tux fit him to perfection, and his brown eyes sought out hers as she waited for her dad to begin walking. There was no doubt in her mind that this was the man she wanted to marry.

As soon as they took their first steps, "Suddenly"—by Billy Ocean—filled the church. Kalissa didn't look at anyone else as she made her descent down the aisle. Nigel shook her dad's hand before grabbing hers.

They said the traditional vows and once it was all over and the preacher pronounced them husband and wife, Nigel kissed her and grabbed her in a bear hug. When they pulled apart, she saw his eyes misting.

"Hey, those are tears of joy, aren't they?" she asked him timidly.

"Yes, lil' mama, you know they are," Nigel smiled and held her close again.

***

Their reception wasn't lavish, but Kalissa was happy with it. There was finger food, drinks, a cake and music. The other table had a wishing well for money, but some people had dropped off gifts on it as well. People milled around, talking to each other, after greeting the bride and groom. No matter how small it was, she was happy, she didn't need any extras. She had changed from her wedding dress into something more comfortable. Nigel still had on his vest, tie and slacks. Kalissa had learned that he loved to dress in suits. Expensive ones, at that.

"Hey, girl! So you did that!" Rayven, her co-worker jumped in her face.

Lissa had heard rumors that that Taj was messing around with Rayven, but he hadn't mentioned her to Kalissa. She had just figured it was a hit it and quit it. When she saw them sitting together at her ceremony, she just shook her head. Rayven looked better than Zandra, but other than that, Lissa couldn't say he had done better. Rayven was an opportunist, and she had various men for different purposes. After the whole Zandra mess, Kalissa steered clear of Taj's affairs.

"Hey! I thought that was you," Lissa gave her a hug and smile of phoniness.

"Yep, you know me and Taj been kicking it. So when he asked me if I wanted to come, I said hell yeah! Girl, you know I am so happy for you!" Rayven gushed.

"Thank you," Kalissa said quietly, looking over Rayven's shoulder for someone to save her. She did not like mixing work with her personal life.

Duke was standing at the bar, by himself and as soon as Lissa spotted him, she disentangled herself from her co-worker.

"Baby D! Why you standing here all by yourself?" Kalissa strutted up to Duke.

"There you are! Every time I tried to say something to you, somebody else had beat me to it." Duke smiled before wrapping her up in a bear hug.

"You here by yourself?" Kaliisa asked him.

"Hell yeah. You bring a woman to a wedding, they think that means you ready!" Duke joked.

"A'ight, mane, don't let that nigga see you hugging his wife like that," Cet joked from behind them.

"You right, you right. But he gots to understand that Lissa is all our sis. Shid, we love her too." Duke released Lissa and shadow-boxed with his cousin.

"Yeah, but she's his wife now. All that shit might change." Cet looked at Lissa expectantly, half joking, half serious.

"I'sa married now." Kalissa twirled around. "But I'ma always be y'all sis. But Cet, you can't hug me like that." She rolled her eyes and laughed.

By this time, Rollo and Fefe had joined them.

"I know damn well Cedric can't hug nobody wit' his short ass. Be trying to suck folks titties and shit," Fefe said in between her laughter.

"Hey, lil' sis, congratulations. I hope Nigel know he got a good one," Rollo said, before handing her an envelope.

"If he doesn't, y'all betta tell him!" Kalissa sang out before giving Rollo a hug. "Where is Dennis?" She looked from Rollo to Fefe.

"I don't know where that fool at. I been calling his ass and he ain't picked up yet," Rollo answered.

"I ain't calling him. We was supposed to have come together and I had to drive myself. That's all I'ma say," Fefe said with an attitude.

Kalissa knew that Dennis and Fefe had been getting close. From what she heard, everything was good.

The DJ played "Never Make a Promise" by Dru Hill.

"That damn Nigel know he love that old music," Rollo laughed.

Nigel sidled up to her, singing a verse, Rod was right behind him.

"Damn, mane, you got the woman now, you can stop all that sanging and shit!" Cet burst out.

"Man, fuck you! I can sing to my woman when I feel like it," Nigel shot back, grabbing Kalissa by the waist, pulling her to him.

Rod laughed so hard, he spat whatever he had been drinking out.

They stood like that while she watched the crowd clear some. Her sister had disappeared, hopefully to pick up their kids, Taj was on the dance floor with Rayven, and Kalissa thought about what Duke said. She hoped that Rayven didn't think her friend was going to marry her run-through ass!

It felt good to have all her friends—old and new— together. It almost felt like old times, but it also reminded Kalissa of how so much had changed. It was time for them to get back together like they used to. Leave all that old pain behind and start off fresh.

Rollo had stepped off to the side on his phone. After hanging up, he looked at them, the anguish clear in his eyes.

"I gotta run. Somebody shot Duck and he's in the hospital in ICU!" Rollo shouted before he ran off, leaving them in shock.

Chapter Twenty-Two

Rod dropped Rollo off at the entrance of Baptist South Emergency Room, and went to park. Rollo ran in, searching for anybody in his family as he passed through the metal detector. The security guard looked at him, processing his custom-made French blue suit with the vest and purple and red paisley tie. Which was in contrast to the worry and anger in his demeanor.

"Renard," his mom approached him from the left corner of the room.

She clutched his arm as he wrapped his arms around her in a tight hug. His mom, Elaine, stood five seven, smooth chocolate-skinned, with two braids hanging down her back. Her coal-black eyes were filled with worry, and mirrored his with anger.

"What's going on, Ma? Where is he?" So many questions plagued Rollo's mind, he shot them off in succession.

With her hand still on his forearm, Elaine pulled him to a corner in the waiting room.

"They are getting him settled in ICU. He can't have visitors for a few hours. I just don't know . . ." Elaine's voice trailed off as tears filled her eyes.

"What happened? I mean, what the hell is going on?" Rollo didn't usually cuss around his mom, but thinking of his baby brother in ICU messed with his head.

"It was that trifling ass hoe Mia! She caused this!" Elaine said furiously in hushed tones.

Confusion lined Rollo's face. "Mia shot Duck? What? How the hell did that happen?"

Mia was definitely bad news, but Rollo couldn't see Duck letting her get the drop on him. Not in any circumstance.

Glancing around the room, his mom stepped closer to him. "She didn't shoot him but I know she sent whoever to shoot him. I kept telling him to leave that bald head ass hoe alone! Why didn't he listen?"

People in the community knew Elaine as a quiet church-going woman who minded her own business and always had a kind word for people. It would have been shocking to them to hear her talk like that, but her sons knew the closer matters were to her heart, the less words she held back. Her children were definitely the only thing that could rile her up.

"Slow down and tell me what you know," Rollo tried to calm her down, because she wasn't making sense.

Elaine cleared her throat. "Dennis went over there and Mia had some boy over there. Obviously, Dennis and Mia had some words and when this punk stepped in, he got his ass beat. Literally. Well, after Dennis left, this sorry ass nigga sent his homeboys to shoot him. They shot my baby three times in the back! In the back, Renard! What kind of coward ass, punk ass niggas would do that?"

No longer able to hold in her tears, Elaine broke down, holding onto her oldest son for dear life. Rollo held her to his chest, trying to calm her down. His mom's entire body shook, which only intensified his wrath.

"Mom, if you haven't seen him yet, how do you know what happened?"

"That boy Jonathan told me. He's the one who brought Dennis to the hospital. If he hadn't been there, my baby probably wouldn't have made it." This thought brought on a fresh set of tears.

Rollo noticed Rod and Fefe had made it inside the waiting room, but he stopped short when he noticed a familiar face walking through the metal detectors.

"What the hell is he doing here?" Rollo murmured.

"Who?" his mom questioned, as she wiped her face with a bandana she'd pulled out of her purse.

Following her son's eyes, she saw the young man he was watching.

"That's Jonathan. I thought you knew him too?" Still dabbing her eyes, she visibly pulled herself together.

"Oh, that's Jojo, Ma, not Jonathan. That's who was wit' Duck?" Tearing his eyes away from Jojo, he looked in his mother's eyes.

"Yeah, he saved your brother's life," Elaine said simply.

After his mom told him that, he noticed that Jojo's tee shirt was covered in blood. He stood in the corner near Rod and Fefe. He noticed Rollo and gave him a look filled with despair.

Rollo motioned him over, and Jojo stood pulling his pants up before slowly walking over. When he made it to Rollo and Elaine, he held his head down. Not only was his shirt covered in blood, but his arms were as well.

"What up, my nigga? Talk to me," Rollo said.

"Well, umm," Jojo began, still looking down.

"Young man! Hold your head up and speak. No one is upset with you, we are so thankful you were there." Elaine spoke to Jojo in a commanding tone.

"Yes, ma'am. Umm, Duck had come over and he was telling me that Mia had called him over to her place. He said that he thought she wanted to make him jealous, cuz she had some dude over there." Jojo paused, still clearly uncomfortable.

"Speak freely, we all fam, ya hear?" Rollo urged him on.

Jojo nodded and continued: "Well, Duck said they got into it and he had bopped her upside the head, when ole dude jumped in and said something. After that, he said that he laid hands on the nigga and left him on the flo'. That's all he told me."

"I'm going to get some water, go ahead and finish," Elaine said.

Rollo knew that his mom, who read people better than anyone he knew, made an exit so that Jojo would speak freely. He respected the youngin for having some semblance of respect for his mom; he just didn't know how real and uncut she was.

"How the fuck some niggas shot my brother, mane? How the fuck both of y'all let them catch y'all slipping like that?" Rollo's tone changed as soon as Elaine was out of earshot.

The real question he wanted answered was how the hell Duck was in the hospital fighting for his life and this nigga didn't have a scratch.

"Mane, when Duck told me how he laid that nigga out and how pissed he was, I went in the spot to get my piece. I know how them scary ass muthafucka's be, so I figured there might be some smoke behind it. As soon as I was trying to make it back out, I heard the shots and ran out. I just didn't expect them to show up there." Jojo's voice remained low but had become animated.

"Where y'all was?" Rollo asked, dread filling his stomach.

"On Erskine, that's why it was so unexpected," Jojo wiped away the tears that snuck out of his eyes.

It made sense to Rollo why Duck had felt comfortable hanging outside without his stick. Erskine was the location of the trap that only a few people knew about. And one of them was Mia. Rollo had stayed on Duck's ass about bringing her there, but he never listened. Heat engulfed his body, and a roaring noise filled his ears. Jojo looked scared as he noticed the vein that bulged across Rollo's forehead. Elaine chose that moment to reappear.

"A'ight, mane, 'preciate ya," Rollo said in dismissal.

"Let me know if you need me," Jojo said, glancing at Elaine.

"Fashow," was all Rollo said.

Elaine watched Jojo walk across the room. She glanced over both shoulders before she spoke. "You know what to do, Renard. Every last one of them niggas. Don't stop until you find every last nigga who was involved. Ya hear?"

"I got this, Ma," Rollo answered, nodding.

"Handle our business, son. But make no mistakes," Elaine said before grabbing him in a hug.

"You might not know who was in that car, but you know who started this. Make sure she never forgets who we are. Mark that bitch fa life," Elaine whispered in her son's ear.

Chapter Twenty-Three

Rollo and Rod sat in the cut where Mia lived. They had changed out of their 'wedding' clothes, and both men wore all black. Rod was quiet, which Rollo appreciated because he hated a talking ass nigga when there was business to take care of. As quiet as Rod was, it still felt weird not to have Duck with him.

Thoughts of his brother brought the images that he could not unsee. Rollo wasn't there, but he knew that once Duck knew that car was aimed at him, he took off in a sprint. And the dirty niggas shot him in the back. His eyes burned, but he refused to let the tears fall.

"Mane, they didn't have to do my bruh like that. Shooting him in the back? Over a fight? About some hoe that don't care about nobody? She just looking for the next dick to ride." Rollo let his frustrations out.

"Mane, these niggas nowadays just pussy. They wanna be gangsters, they don't realize who to fuck wit' and who not to fuck wit'." Rod responded.

Rollo studied him. "You shole right, that's the truth. They done fucked wit' the wrong one this time. I really hate to make an example outta muthafuckas, but this time they forced my hand. Dis shit is personal."

"Look like this bitch ain't never coming home. You checked on yo' mom?" Rod said, leaning his seat back.

"Nah, my lil' brothers up there wit' her. And I told Jojo not to leave just in case somebody try something. She straight. And she ain't gonna leave that hospital for no—" Rollo stopped short, when a car pulled into the parking lot.

"There she go, right there." Rollo leaned forward in his seat.

The beat-up grey Nissan Sentra parked, and the passenger door flew open first. A skinny dude with auburn tips on his half-twisted hair jumped out.

"Pull up behind them! My muthfuckin' brother laid up in the hospital and this bitch still riding this nigga around!" Rollo roared.

Rod hit the gas and with gravel and dust kicking up behind them, he stopped the car behind Mia's. The skinny guy looked over his shoulder and, when he saw Rod and Rollo, ran to the stairway.

"You get his ass and let me handle dis hoe," Rollo instructed.

Rod took off behind Mia's boyfriend while Rollo strolled to the driver's side of Mia's car. He heard her locks click and at the same time heard the splintering sound of her apartment door being kicked in.

Mia looked frightened as she stared through her dirty car window.

"Get out the car, Mia," Rollo told her.

Mia shook her head fearfully, and her eyes grew wide as Rollo pulled out his piece.

"I'm not gonna tell yo' ass again. Get out the fucking car!"

Mia's held her shaking hands up. "Don't shoot me!" she yelled.

"Just put the gun down and I'll get out, please?" Mia had tears streaming down her face as she negotiated.

Rollo stuck his gun in the back of his pants and held his hands out to show her. As soon as Mia opened the door, he snatched her by her wig and threw her down on the ground.

"This what you want, bitch?"

Mia tried to scramble away when Rollo kicked her in the face. As she hollered loudly, he grabbed her by her hair again and dragged her through the parking lot to the sidewalk. Not caring about the debris, glass and rocks that littered the ground.

"Freek! Help me, Freek! Please stop, oh please stop!" Mia yelled, her face swelling from the brunt of his shoe.

"Nah, bitch you wasn't telling yo' little boyfriend to stop when he shot my brother. You think that lil' nigga want some of this?" Rollo growled as he pulled her to her feet.

"I didn't know! I didn't want anything to happen," was all she was able to get out before Rollo punched her in the face.

Once again on the ground, Mia tried to crawl back to her car. The pain she was feeling was obvious in the way she moved. Mia tried one last tactic to save her life.

"Rollo, please! I'm pregnant, it's Duck's," she managed get out as blood seeped out of her busted mouth.

"Hoe, ain't no seed from my family coming through yo' raggedy ass," Rollo said before kicking her twice in the stomach.

Howling, Mia curled up in the fetal position. Some neighbors had come out, and many more peeked out their windows, but this was Rollo's hood. Not only did he serve there, he had grown up there. So, when people realized it was him, they gawked but no one would call twelve or get involved.

Rollo looked inside her car, and found her cell phone in the middle console. He grabbed it and smashed it beneath his feet on the sidewalk.

Mia was left moaning and lying on the ground as he strode to her apartment. Rod stood at the door when Rollo walked in. The skinny guy, Aaron, sat on the dirty sofa, glowering at Rod. When Rollo walked in, his eyes grew huge.

"Mane, I don't know what that bitch ass nigga told you, but we didn't steal no dope off him, Rollo. That was on a personal tip. I know he ya man's and all but he acted like I was something to play wit'. Me and my boys, we ain't 'bout that shit! We don't play, we laying niggas down. Dats all." Aaron stuck his chest out.

Rollo walked over to him and jabbed him with a left hook that knocked him down. In a rage he yelled: "Nigga, you think I'm busting up in here about some dope? Y'all muthafuckas shot my brother in the back. About a hoe that when you ain't around she gonna give up to any nigga that tell her ugly ass she cute. You proud of that pussy ass shit?"

"Yo' b-b-brother?" Aaron stuttered, sitting up with fear crowding his eyes.

Rollo laid him out again with another left hook. "And y'all think you killas? Huh, nigga? Look me in my eyes and kill me, pussy!" Rollo roared thumping his chest.

He pulled Aaron up. "C'mon, show me what you got."

Aaron's eye had closed up. His lip and nose were swollen. Snot ran down to his trembling lips as he cried, "Mane, I didn't know that was yo' brother. I promise!"

"Yo ass know it now. Even if he wasn't I hate pi ass niggas like y'all. Running around shooting out of fucking cars, cuz yo' ass can't fight! About nothing. A hoe that still going be hoeing before yo' ass get cold. I promise you if my bruh wanted to kill ya, you would be dead," Rollo told him.

Aaron's entire body shook with fear. "Shid, I wasn't even the one who shot him, I swear I didn't. That was Poochie ass!"

"Poochie? Who the fuck is Poochie?"

"Mane, he Blood like me. His ass crazy. I just told him what happened and I didn't even know what he was planning. When we saw Duck and Poochie pulled out that choppa, it was too late." Aaron talked fast, speckling the carpet with blood with each word.

Rollo glanced back at Rod. "Aye, mane, go make sure that hoe still on the ground outchea."

"Say less, my nigga." Rod walked out the door.

Rollo turned back to Aaron. "Poochie just fucked you up, my nigga. This shit you talking don't mean nothing to me."

Aaron stood looking around, but before he could make a move, Rollo stepped over to him, putting a hand on each side of his head and snapped his neck.

"That's real nigga shit," Rollo spat on Aaron while his body spasmed on the floor. He walked out the door without glancing back.

Rod was leaning on his ride while Mia was just trying to get off the ground. An older lady was trying to help her and she looked at Rollo with fear in her eyes when he walked out. Rollo put his hand on his piece as he looked at her, but with all the older people standing outside, and gave Mia a parting shot.

"Aight, Mia, you might want to get yo'self checked out."

Rollo pulled out his phone when he got inside Rod's car. "Aye, mane, you know Poochie that's a Blood? Yo, this nigga be hanging with a nigga they call Freek," Rollo said to whoever he had called.

156

He nodded before speaking again: "Yeah, that's him. Where he be hanging? Oh yeah?" He paused again. "Umm-hmm, yeah, I know exactly where you talking 'bout. Whereabouts he live?"

Rollo listened intently. "Word? You talm 'bout Sadie from Smiley Cote? That's her lil' brother?"

After a brief pause, Rollo spoke into the receiver again. "Preciate you, bruh. I'll holla at ya later."

He put the phone in his lap and looked at Rod.

"Let's ride and get at this nigga real quick," he said quietly.

"Bet," was Rod's only response.

Following Rollo's direction, the men headed towards the airport. They stopped at the gas station about two miles of the airport. The place looked closed, but there were four cars in the parking lot.

"Turn yo' lights off before you pull in," Rollo said, sitting up in the passenger seat, casing the place out.

There was an older fixed up Caprice Classic with a lone man standing at the back of it.

"Ain't that Boo Man?" Rod asked.

"Yeah, that's his fat ass. Pull up beside him," Rollo answered.

"What it do, my nigga?" Rollo asked after letting his window down.

"Mane, what up witcha?" Boo Man asked, stuffing a roll of money in his pocket.

"Not a damn thang. What you doing out here?"

"Just finished robbing them niggas in a dice game." Boo Man pointed towards the left side of the building. "They so fucked up they don't know if they rolling doubles or not." Boo Man laughed.

"That nigga Poochie back there?" Rollo asked, looking the way Boo Man pointed.

"Hell yeah, that's who I just robbed. I was 'bout to leave befo' that nigga realize how light his pocket is."

"Who else back there?"

"Poochie, Lil Doot and one other nigga, I didn't catch his name," Boo Man laughed. "I just call him broke."

"But you sure that's Poochie the Blood that run wit' Freek back there?" Rollo asked again.

"Yeah, mane, his crazy ass back there."

Rollo reached up under the seat and pulled the Draco out. Boo Man's eyes got big as he took a few steps back.

"I guess you need to take yo' ass on then," Rollo said slowly.

"Yeah, mane. I'll holla," Boo Man said, almost tripping to get in his car.

Rod watched Rollo rummage through his book bag until he pulled out a black stocking cap. He looked at Rod and winked.

"I'll be right back, keep the motor running," Rollo said, sliding the stocking cap on.

"Mane, I know you don't think I'ma sit here while you go by yo'self!" Rod argued.

"Mane, I got this. I need you to watch my back. This ain't no Desert Storm, dis mo' like Sandcastles. Just keep yo' eyes open and the motor running."

Rod mumbled as he pulled out his Glock. Rollo slid out the car silently without shutting the door completely. Rollo held the rifle close to his side. Rod frowned when he saw him go towards the right of the store. One quick turn away from Rollo, then when he looked back he was gone. Rod cracked his door open, but before he could get out, he heard the Draco going off.

Plltt! Plltt! Pllftt! Pllfft! Pllfftt!

Rod put his foot back in the car and closed his door, still holding his Glock. He strained his eyes, looking at both ends of the store, not knowing who was going to come out. Within a few minutes, Rollo came around the left side, still moving quickly and got back in the car.

"Them niggas didn't try to draw on you?" Rod asked as he burned rubber, pulling off.

Rollo moved from side to side with the motion of the vehicle.

"Naw, the only one that saw me was facing me. By the time he realized I was back there, that nigga was dead," Rollo said after spitting out the window.

"Was that Poochie?" Rod asked with a sideways glance at his passenger.

"Hell if I know. It was Poochie and 'em. I jus' know he was one of them and dats good enough for me. Whoever the rest of them country ass pussies was, they was guilty by association." Rollo leaned back in his seat and closed his eyes.

Chapter Twenty-Four

Taj and Cet sat at the reception, watching the last few stragglers hang around. Rayven had left Taj and stood with Kalissa by the wishing well table, motioning with her hands as if she was saying something important. Kalissa continued to put the gifts in a bag.

"Mane, I hate that shit happened to Duck! I hope he be alright. And I feel sorry for whoever did that shit," Cet said, placing both hands behind his head.

"I know. Did you know he was Rollo's brother?" Taj asked, still keeping his eyes on Rayven.

Sitting up and looking at Taj, Cet said excitedly: "Nah, I knew they were close and I guess whoever did that shit didn't know either. They couldn't have. That nigga 'bout to paint this city red. Especially if he don't make it."

"Mane, I'm glad niggas don't be coming for us like that." Taj's voice was quiet and serious.

"That's because of Unc'! Other than Desi and we still don't know who did that shit. I think it was them niggas from Applebee's and if I ever see them again it's on. Cuz Desi and Duke stood on all ten in front of them." Cet's voice rose with each word.

"You think they came for Duck cuz they ain't wit Unc', no mo'?" Taj's eyebrows shot up.

Cet looked surprised by the thought, he rubbed his chin, "Mane, I didn't even think of that. Maybe so, but they still fucked up. Big time."

"It was good to see Duke, I ain't seen that nigga in a minute. I thought he had left town." Taj laughed, trying to lighten the mood.

"Shid, after Desi that nigga don't fuck wit' none of us! He's back in school, trying to get that paper. He got the hell up outta here when he heard about Duck. He probably think we death and destruction now." Cet shook his head.

"I'm kinda glad he got out, but the nigga could've said bye!" Taj laughed, feeling the liquor he was drinking.

Cet laughed too. "More like kiss his ass!" Cet took another look around the clubhouse. "Buttt why yeen tell me that Duck and Fefe was kicking it?"

"I didn't know for real. I seen them together a few times, but I didn't think nothing 'bout it."

"Damn! All the good women gone! Lissa done got married, I tole yo' ass once I saw that nigga sanging and shit, that they wasn't breaking up. Now look, he done married her! Ain't nothing left in our crew but the chickenheads," Cet said, looking towards Rayven.

Taj laughed, "Don't be slick dissing my woman. She's alright for real."

Cet's eyes said it all before he opened his mouth. "Mane, just yesterday, she wasn't yo' woman and now she is? Mane, you better be careful. You know we making mo' chedda and some of these women are just about what they can get." Cet looked down and mumbled. "Like that stack you gave her yesterday."

"Nah, she ain't like that. She's cool and she really cares. Not like Zandra's ass always having her hand out. Rayven didn't ask me to buy her something, I offered. There's a difference."

"Mane, you always trying to get hemmed up! Why don't you just fuck around some? Yo' ass always trying to have a woman. Shid, I keep one on every side of town and that ain't counting my baby mommas. Even though I don't really fuck them no more." Cet was animated.

"Shid, you spend mo' money wit' mo than one. I ain't 'bout that life. Bitches be wanting you to get their hair nails and doggone feet done! That's enough money fo' just one." Taj laughed.

"Fa real tho', you asked Lissa 'bout her? I mean they been working together for a while," Cet continued trying to get his point across.

"Nah, mane! Lissa ain't my momma! You see they get along pretty good," Taj said, slowly moving his eyes back to where the women stood.

"You call that getting along? Lissa look like she about to cuss ole girl out," Cet laughed into his hand.

"I think she's just worried about Duck. You know they have gotten close lately. Her Rollo, Rod and Duck," Taj mumbled.

"Humph, I didn't know that. I'm surprised Nigel lets her get close to anyone." Cet's eyes found Nigel standing a few feet away from Lissa, talking to her cousin or somebody.

"You know they all grew up in The Village. That's probably why he trust them niggas. And you know Rod is his cousin. Anyway, I think that's why she looking like that."

Cet grabbed his cup from under his seat. He looked at Taj over the rim, but the crinkles in his eyes made it evident he was smiling. "You done let them niggas take yo' place? Damn!"

"Fuck you, nigga. They ain't close like that!" Taj frowned before changing the subject.

***

Kalissa hung up from Fefe as Nigel pulled into the loop of the hotel. With their work schedules and lack of funds, a trip had been out of the question. Nigel had mumbled about it, but Kalissa was fine with it. Of course, her sister had something to say about it, chastising Kalissa for making Nigel leave the streets.

"What did Fefe say? How is he?" Nigel asked.

"She's not sure, he's still in ICU but they finally let his mom go back there with him," Kalissa said slowly.

"Damn! I hate that happened. Did Rollo get to go back and see him?"

"Fefe said Rollo and Rod left shortly after she got there. I guess they will be back soon." Kalissa cocked her head towards Nigel. He just raised his eyebrows because the valet had walked up.

The suite was nice! A lump formed in her throat when Nigel carried her in, because rose petals lined the floor from the door to the bedroom. Nigel dumped her on the bed, which was also filled with red rose petals.

"You did this?" Kalissa squealed as she got up and began jumping up and down on the bed.

"Who else you think did it? The tooth fairy?" Nigel's voice was muffled because he sat on the edge of bed, taking his shoes off.

Lissa jumped on his back, wrapping her arms around his neck. "You love me!"

"Lissa, get off me!" Nigel laughed, trying to dump her off.

"You think cuz you my husband now, you can tell me what to do?" Lissa joked, still hanging on his neck.

"Shid, I already know that won't happen," Nigel laughed as he stood.

Nigel began spinning around, while she screamed for him to stop. He dumped her once again on the bed. Kalissa jumped back up, a little wobbly and began jumping on the bed again.

"We is married! We is married! You belong to me and I belong to you! Forever,' she chanted while Nigel looked on with a smile.

Out of steam, she finally laid down on her side with her hand holding her head.

"Nigel, it seems like every time we have a good time and some happiness, some bullshit happens. I hope Duck is alright, but I can't lie, my first thought was that I am so glad you are not in that life anymore. I swear. I don't know what I would do if I got a call like that. Every night you were out late, that thought crossed my mind."

Nigel laid across the bed beside her. Taking her hand in his and kissing it, he looked her in her eyes. "I was thinking the same thing. I mean, don't get me wrong, I get tired of us struggling, but I rather be able to come home to you and the kids in one piece."

Those words made Kalissa's heart swell with love. She thought that Nigel resented her for asking him to leave the streets. To know that he didn't resent her meant the world to her.

"It won't always be a struggle, as long as we do it together, we'll be alright," Kalissa murmured while taking off her clothes.

Nigel kissed her nose. "As smart as you are, I'm sure you gonna have a plan." He rolled his eyes. "That's according to Rod."

Kalissa giggled first, then turned serious. "I hope him and Rollo don't get hurt. Rollo was so upset, so he might not be thinking straight." A sigh escaped from Kalissa's lips. "By the way, we got two gees in the wishing well," she told him, not mentioning the one gee Rollo had slipped her.

"Aw shucks now! What we gonna do wit' that?" Nigel smiled.

"We gonna get caught up on some bills first, then we'll see," she smiled back at him.

"Whateva. What else you got for me?"

Kalissa started rolling her panties down. Nigel's face filled with lust as he watched her. His dick sprang out of his boxers before she removed her panties. Kalissa moved slowly, never taking her eyes off his, except to look at his dick. When he began stroking his dick, she wet her lips with her tongue.

"That shit right there, turn me the fuck on!" she whispered.

"Come on let me take yo' temperature," Nigel growled.

Kalissa crawled over on all fours to where he stood. Her tongue snaked out, with the tip tracing the edge of his head, then sliding down, almost to his balls. Nigel's hands were in her hair, really making her wet. After going down on him, she stopped caressing his balls to take them in her mouth, sucking them softly. Then her tongue slipped down below, making him gasp.

Nigel pulled her up by her hair, kissing her roughly before laying her down. He pushed both of her knees into her shoulder and slid right into her wetness. Lissa threw back at him, gently at first until she got one leg free, then she gave it all to him. Every time he pulled out enough for her to feel his fat head, violins struck a chord in her head.

Nigel pulled out with a loud wet plop and turned her over on her stomach. Lissa poked her ass back, throwing it back to catch each long stroke. When he popped her ass, a river let loose and by the third slap her body tensed up as she felt him make his shaky deposit.

After a short nap, they woke up for two more rounds. One in the bathroom, and one on the dining table.

They were married for real then! Consummated and all!

C.D. Blue

Chapter Twenty-Five

Two Weeks Later

"Guhl! I wish I had known about Rod's cookout, I would have gotten Mariah to cover for me," Rayven complained when she came in to relieve Kalissa.

Lissa internally rolled her eyes. What Rayven didn't realize was that she purposely put her on the schedule, so that she couldn't go to the cookout. Work people and her social life did not mix. Rayven talked too much, and Lissa did not need to be 'on the clock' while she was trying to have fun.

"Yeah, I hate you gonna miss it. Don't worry, Rod will have another one," Kalissa said lightly.

"I know, but Taj is so hyped about this one. You should've seen him when I told him I had to work. He was like a sad puppy," Rayven laughed.

Another internal eye roll from Kalissa. Instead, she murmured, "Aww, how cute. Girl! Let me go, I gotta pick up my kids and get them ready. You need anything else before I go?"

"Naw, have fun. Let me know if Taj bring anybody else," Rayven said to her back.

When Kalissa looked back at her, she laughed, covering her mouth. "I'm jus' playing. I trust him."

Finally, with her purse on her shoulder, Lissa made it to the door only to be stopped again by Rayven.

"Kalissa!" Rayven yelled.

With a deep breath, Kalissa turned around to find Rayven right in her face.

"I forgot to tell you that Brian's brother, remember the fine one? He came in here the other day with Taj's ex-girlfriend! They was all hugged up and shit. I said to myself how she managed to hook up wit' him? Did you introduce them?" Rayven reveled in the gossip she was telling.

"Nah, I didn't, but I wish them the best," Kalissa said with a small smile. "See you tomorrow."

When Kalissa got in her car, she breathed heavily and her professional mask disappeared like magic. Hitting her hand against the steering wheel, she thought about Zandra and Malachi. All she could hope was that Fefe hadn't shared anything with that bitch when Lissa was with Brian. Racking her brain, she tried to remember all that she had told her friend. The only thing she could remember was that white picket fence fairy tale.

Backing out of the parking space, it dawned on her that she had also joked about faking anger to get to Fefe's house. Lissa remembered how hard Fefe had laughed at her false indignation about Brian pulling her arm.

With a shrug, she drove to the daycare, determined not to let the past interfere with her fun. Moving her shoulders to "Shawty" by Plies, she turned her thoughts away from Malachi and that entire dreadful business. She wished he would just go away. And take Zandra with his ass. Damn!

***

Rod had just moved into a house off Narrow Lane and was having a cookout to celebrate. Lissa was so happy for him and Leaisha. He was doing big things and making the right moves. He had everything laid out. Plenty of food, beer, liquor and gas! The perfect party!

Kalissa looked around, seeing Taj, Cet, Jojo. Her smile faded some when she saw Jojo and some other guy she didn't know.

A genuine smile crossed her face as she hoped Fefe would break away from Duck to come. The bullets had missed his spine but still did damage. Duck had to rehab four days a week to help him walk again. Fefe was there every step of the way. Kalissa was happy her friend had finally found love.

Rollo walked into the backyard, wearing all black. A fitted tee that matched his jeans, with his dreads in two French braids. He had a woman with him. Intrigued, Lissa sat up straight because this was the first time she had ever seen him with a woman. She was a pretty mixed looking chick with curly hair, and she wore a yellow strapless maxi dress which didn't hide that she was chunky.

Interested, Lissa kept her eyes on them but didn't approach until after everyone finished approaching him and they went to the food table.

She walked up behind him, standing on tiptoe to whisper in his ear, "You going out on a mission tonight?"

Rollo turned and burst out into a huge smile. "Hey, lil' sis! Shid, not tonight, at least I don't think so." He winked.

Little Miss Mixed stood there with a stank look on her face. Rollo turned and introduced the two women.

"Hey, Lissa, this is Paris," he said before stuffing his face with macaroni and cheese.

"Hey," was all Paris said, still looking at Kalissa with the stank look.

"Hi," was all Lissa offered back.

"Damn! This mac and cheese is the shit. You gotta try this," Rollo exclaimed, addressing Paris.

"Umm-hmm, so you like my recipe?" Lissa grinned.

"You did this? Damn, who knew your lil' ass could cook." Rollo laughed, piling more on his plate.

"Don't you work at Applebee's?" Paris asked Lissa.

"Yes, I sure do. Why?" Lissa was tired of this little princess.

"I just thought you looked familiar, me and my sorors go there all the time. You look different without your uniform," Paris said with a smirk.

Kalissa stood there, trying to figure out if Paris was trying to be smart or not. Then she noticed Paris looking her up and down, with her nose turned up. Kalissa had her two baby flat stomach on blast with a deep blue criss-crossed bralette and a short skirt that flowed above her knees.

"Umm, that's weird because you don't look familiar to me. I guess because once you've seen one set of drunk sorors, they all look alike. I'll holla at you later, Ro," Kalissa said before walking off.

"Hey lil' mama, what you doing sitting here by yo'self?" Nigel whispered in her ear after she sat back down.

"Just thinking about slapping a bitch for trying to act like she better than me," Lissa huffed.

Nigel laughed. "Who the hell trying to act better than my baby?"

"That heifer with Rollo. Talm about I look different without my uniform! Cuz her and her sorority sisters come in there all the time! Like that's supposed to mean something." Lissa's brow furrowed more with each word.

"I'm sure she didn't mean anything by it," Nigel chuckled, taking a swig out of his beer bottle.

Lissa cut her eyes to the side at him. "Don't you never take up for another bitch to me."

Nigel widened his eyes, clearly laughing around the beer bottle. "Oh, you so violent, lil' mama. You know that shit turns me on."

"What y'all over here looking so serious about?" Rod came up.

"Yo' bro 'bout to get his head busted to the white meat. Taking another woman's side," Kalissa deadpanned, before she laughed.

"Naw! Nigga you know I taught you betta than that," Rod faked looking shocked.

"He obviously forgot," Lissa rolled her eyes.

"Whose side you taking, mane?" Rod popped Nigel with the towel he held.

"Ion even know. The heifer with Rollo." Nigel emphasized the last sentence.

"Oh, her. I don't know this one, she must be new," Rod said, glancing over towards Rollo and Paris.

"New? I ain't never seen him with a woman until today. Why he chose that one? I have no clue!" Lissa shook her head.

"That's how you know he a true playa. You hardly ever see him wit' a woman, but you know he got one or two or three," Rod whispered.

"Mane, you can't be giving her the game," Nigel laughed.

"Naw now, I needed to know that. Wherever you go, I shall follow. Let all the bitches know Lissa is in the house!" Lissa had stood in her chair, yelling and waving her arms. Nigel caught her before she fell off.

"Mane, y'all tripping. Let me go help my baby. Don't start no fights at my new spot. Alright?" Rod looked at Kalissa.

"No worries. I'm used to the hatorade," Lissa winked.

The next thing they heard was Rod on the mike, "I'm playing the next ole school track in honor of my brother, Nigel and his wife Lissa, who is now my sister. Y'all get up and dance, nigga."

"Never Make a Promise", by Dru Hill, floated through the air. Nigel and Kalissa got up to dance, but Nigel grabbed the mike and began singing. He grabbed Lissa by the waist as they rocked to the love song. Nigel gave her a sloppy kiss at the end, letting her know that this was going to be a good night later.

The rest of the night went well, they drank, smoked, danced and finally played cards! Fefe showed up, but only stayed for a short time. She was there long enough for her and Lissa to talk about the new girl on the block, Paris. Taj left in time to pick Rayven up from work; Lissa was still tickled about how she set that up. Cet seemed to hook up with Leashia's cousin, Monique, and Jojo sat around looking like he was mad at the world, as usual.

Just another night with the crew!

Chapter Twenty-Six

For some odd reason, Kalissa woke up early. Probably because of going to work early after partying Friday night. Then they went back to Rod's the next night. It was just the four of them, Rod, Leaisha, Kalissa, Nigel and the kids. No drama, just fun.

The sun peeped in through the curtains, and the morning just felt fresh. As much as she usually hated getting up before eight on her off days, she enjoyed the quiet of the early morning. Her grandmother had come to her again last night. Kalissa mulled over her words. *"People are drawn to your strength. Being strong is like beauty, it's a blessing and a curse."*

This was one that the younger version of her grams had gotten wrong! It seemed as if more people were turned off from her strength versus being drawn to it. Opening the curtains and blinds, she decided she would cook breakfast.

As soon as she had gotten the turkey bacon, pancake mix and cooking oil out, the doorbell rang. Lissa's stomach churned because she felt it was too early for anyone to stopping by. Peeping out the window, she saw Rollo. Disregarding her shorts and tee shirt, she swung the door open.

"Ro, what's wrong?" Lissa cried as she let him in. Rollo looked as if he had been up all night.

"Where's Nigel?" Rollo asked, his voice shaking.

Before she answered, he said words she never wanted to hear.

"He's gone, lil' sis. They got him, he's gone," Rollo croaked.

"Who? Who's gone?" Kalissa asked, bewildered.

"Rod, lil' sis. They shot him down last night." Rollo's voice still shook, and he had tears in his eyes.

Time stopped, and the wind left Lissa's body. All of a sudden it appeared as if she was looking at everything through a foggy glass. A huge stomach cramp hit her, and she held her stomach as if that would stop the pain flowing through her body.

"No, that can't be right. That can't be right. What? Who? I mean why? Why would somebody do that?" Kalissa asked no one in particular.

"I don't know, I wish I could tell you." Rollo shook his head, looking sorrowful.

"I can't tell Nigel, no I can't do it," she whispered, wringing her hands.

"Tell me what?" Nigel's deep voice, still full of sleep boomed behind her.

Kalissa and Rollo looked at one another, then back to Nigel. Rollo spoke first.

"It's Rod, mane, he gone. Them muthafuckas shot him in front of his house."

"Nooooo," Nigel's scream was heart wrenching. He fell to the floor on one knee as Kalissa and Rollo grabbed him and lifted him up.

"Tell me you lying, man, not Rod, not my brother," Nigel yelled. His tears flowed freely, without shame or consequence.

"Mane, I wish I was," Rollo said quietly.

The hot tears that scalded Kalissa's throat rushed out after seeing her husband in so much pain. She grabbed him around his waist, and he held her tightly.

"Lil' mama, he can't be gone. We was just talking the other day. Nooo, mane, this shit can't be happening!" Nigel cried, the stomp of his foot shaking the entire room.

Kalissa didn't know what to say, she just cried with him. They both felt Rollo's arms around them as they fell apart, and the three of them created of circle of hurt. Their tears created a connection that they all felt but would not realize the power of that bond until much later.

***

"Girl, you do what's best for you. All the family has an opinion, but your name is on that paperwork. When it comes time to pay bills, all them niggas will be ghosts," Kalissa held the phone to her ear as she cooked and talked to Leaisha at the same time.

"That's mine!" Justin ran behind Jamila, screaming about a toy she had.

"Hold on for a minute. Y'all stop running in this house before I get the belt! Jamila, whatever you took, give it back to him!" Kalissa yelled at her children. "Okay, I'm back."

Kalissa had been talking to Leaisha daily, trying to help figure out funeral arrangements. Rod didn't have life insurance and, although James and Rollo had taken care of the expenses Leaisha was left with handling the arrangements. Rod's mom had been on drugs for most of his life, so she wasn't much help.

"I just don't know what to do. I don't want his family mad at me, but I also don't want to be stuck with bills I can't pay," Leaisha cried. "Not only that, but I also don't want to live in that house! I tried to go there today to get his stuff, and I couldn't do it. All I could see was him lying behind his car and all that blood." She paused, sniffling. "I told his mom she could go get his stuff and clean out his belongings," Leaisha told Kalissa before she started crying again. "I just can't, I mean, my dad had to go clear my stuff out. I still can't believe this shit is happening."

"I know, me too. It still feels like a bad dream," Kalissa muttered truthfully.

In the week since Rod's death, everything had changed. Nigel alternated between laying in bed, not talking or doing anything, to hanging out getting drunk. Kalissa didn't know what to say or do. He wasn't going to work. She had left work early twice to go with Leaisha to the funeral home. If this kept up, she and Nigel would be out in the streets soon. Kalissa immediately felt bad for having those thoughts.

"Don't feel bad, that's perfectly understandable. It's just a hard time for everybody," Lissa told her.

"I know, but then they keep asking me why was he outside, where was I, had we been arguing, and all kinds of crazy shit," Leaisha voice cracked. "They acting like I had something to do with this!"

Kalissa loved Rod, but his family was another story. They had carried on so bad at the funeral home before Rollo and James came. She was just embarrassed. Hearing what they had been saying made her snap.

175

"Girl, fuck them folks! Don't let them get in yo' head. Just don't answer their calls," Kalissa advised.

"I wish I could do that, but it just ain't in me."

"Humph, I would've been—" Lissa stopped when she heard Nigel come in on the phone. "Hey, let me call you back. Nigel just got home."

Kalissa hung up and looked at Nigel as their kids surrounded him. He hung up from his call after saying, "Let me see what Lissa says and I'll let you know."

Once the children settled down, she asked him, "What you need to ask me?"

"Huh?" Nigel snapped.

"I heard what you said on the phone," Lissa tried to be patient.

"Oh, that was San, Rod's mom. She wants us to go get his stuff out of the house." Nigel was still frowning.

"Damn! She's so trifling! She acts like she can't do shit! She wasn't no kind of mother in his life and she can't help out now?" Lissa snapped.

"I know. She said it's too much for her," Nigel said slowly.

Lissa looked at the television, willing her heart to get to a better place. She did not want to go to the house either! That would make this nightmare a reality. When she looked away from the television, Nigel was staring at her.

"Okay, let's do it in the morning after the kids go to daycare," she said softly giving in.

The next morning, they got to Rod's house after dropping the kids off. Dried blood was still in the driveway, marking the spot it happened. The muscle in Nigel's jaw ticked furiously, but he squared his shoulders and marched past it. Kalissa stood there looking at it for a minute with tears and vomit in her throat. She followed her husband.

Everything looked much the same, Kalissa could tell what Leaisha's dad had taken. Nothing major. All the knick knacks and pictures were gone. As she moved to the kitchen, she noticed the pots and pans were gone. All the furniture, except the one in Leaisha's daughter's room, was still there.

"I talked to Rollo, he's getting a truck to get the furniture this evening. I think San just wants his clothes and shit," Nigel said.

They walked to the bedroom. Once Nigel saw Rod's clothes in the closet, his leg began shaking and he bit his bottom lip.

"Baby, why don't you go to the den and check outside for his things. I'll take care of this," Kalissa said softly, touching his arm.

Nigel nodded and went out. Kalissa started with the dresser. She pulled out all of his clothes and underwear, and placed them on the bed. Realizing she needed to put them in something, she walked to kitchen to get some trash bags. Nigel was standing in the den, holding a picture of Rod, crying silently. Kalissa's heart broke, but she knew the sooner they left the better. She grabbed the box.

Stuffing the shorts, tee shirts and underwear in bags, she looked to the closet. His jeans jackets and two heavy garment bags went on the bed next. She took everything off the hangers and pushed them into another bag.

Rod had a million shoes! Kalissa pulled another bag out to put them in. After one bag full, she threw the rest on the bedroom floor, deciding to bag them up last. Behind the shoes were three large suitcases. Kalissa shook her head.

"I could've put all the clothes in these."

When she pulled on the first one, it wouldn't budge.

"What the hell?" Kalissa murmured. She pulled the zipper down and got the surprise of her life! The suitcase was full of bags of blow! Going to the next one, she unzipped it; it was filled with cases of pills! The third was full of weed.

Lissa's eyes bulged and her hands shook. With narrowed eyes she glanced back at the heavy garment bags she'd thrown on the bed earlier. Tiptoeing over to the bed, she unzipped the first bag. Bands of cash, mostly hundreds, fell out! Kalissa covered her mouth with her hands, her mind moving a thousand miles per second.

"Nigel! Nigel, come here!" she yelled.

His footsteps thumped to the back. "What? What happened?" Nigel stopped short when he saw the cash.

Kalissa walked to the closet and dragged out one of the suitcases. "And look at what else?"

"Damn! Mane, he must have just done a pick up! We've got to get that shit back to them folks." Nigel grabbed his head in frustration.

Kalissa looked at him slyly. "Wait, not so fast. I have a plan."

Chapter Twenty-Seven

The day of the funeral was beautiful and sunny. The kids had stayed with her sister the night before so she and Nigel got dressed quietly. Nigel looked sad but so handsome in his dark blue suit, complete with a vest and a silk blue paisley tie with a tinge of burgundy. Kalissa wore a blue and white sleeveless pencil dress, with burgundy six-inch heels. Nigel had picked it out for her when they went shopping the night before.

She walked up to him and gave him a kiss. "I know today will be hard but I'm going to be right beside you."

"I know, baby. I just can't believe we are about to bury Rod. I keep trying to wake up from this and I can't. That man wasn't my cousin, he was my brother." Nigel rubbed his eyes.

"I know, baby, I know." Kalissa placed her forehead against his.

"Alright, let's do this," Nigel sighed dejectedly.

The service was at the funeral home since Rod didn't have a church. It seemed as if all the streets of Montgomery turned out. It was packed. Nigel and Kalissa walked in with the family to view Rod's body. Nigel leaned over and kissed his cousin's forehead, then turned to Kalissa. She stood there looking at Rod, memorializing his face in her heart. No way was she kissing a dead body, though! She followed Nigel to their seats.

Kalissa sat in between Nigel and Leaisha, bringing memories back of Desi's funeral. She was tired of burying her friends and family, they were too young to be dying like this. Tears leaked from her eyes as a young lady and young man sang "One Sweet Day" by Mariah Carey. As soon as the first lyrics came out of her mouth, Leaisha started bawling. Nigel's leg was bouncing like crazy, and Kalissa just put her arms around both of them.

After that the eulogy, which was too long and had nothing to do with Rod, since the preacher didn't know him, people seemed restless. Then they were all surprised by a guest speaker. It was Duke.

"Umm, for those of you who don't know me, I am Adonis Thatcher but most people call me Duke." He looked around the crowded chapel and cleared his throat before continuing. "It seems like only a little while ago, I was at another service for my brother, Desi. If someone had told me then, that, one: I would be speaking at any funeral, I wouldn't have believed it. Two: if I ever thought I would be speaking at this man's funeral, I also wouldn't have believed it."

Duke pulled a handkerchief out of his pocket and wiped his eyes. "No, I didn't know Rod as well as many of you here. But I knew him. The main reason I wanted to speak was because the last time I saw Rod, his words impacted my life. It was a few weeks ago, and he told me that he was proud of me."

While his words mesmerized Kalissa, she could tell how hard Nigel was trying to hold back his tears. She squeezed his thigh reassuringly. As for Leaisha, she let hers out. Loudly.

"Now I'm about to keep this real and if I offend anybody, I'm apologizing now. I know some of y'all are saying what's such a big deal about him being proud of you? Me, like many of you, I only wanted to be the big man in the streets, for as long as I can remember. Me and my brother," Duke's voice broke and he once again wiped his face. "We used to talk about all the cars we would have, the women and things we would buy for our mom. So, when it finally started happening, we were happy. And when my brother died in my arms, I still wanted to go harder. And I wanted revenge. I was determined to get my lick back."

Wiping the tears from his eyes unashamedly, Duke paused again. This time longer. Somebody in the audience yelled out: "Come on, mane, preach!"

This made others murmur in agreement. Kalissa saw the older woman sitting with Rollo raise her arms and then she shouted, "Baby, finish yo' testimony! Somebody here needs to hear it!"

Duke nodded and continued: "Then somebody dear to me told me to get out of the streets. That didn't mean anything to me, I'd heard that a million times. But when they said don't make yo' momma go through this again. That hit home. I thought about seeing my mom hold my dead brother and thinking that her tears, pain and heartbeat could bring him back. That's something I'll never forget. I realized they were right. My momma didn't deserve to go through that the first time, definitely not twice. So, I left. Knowing that the streets are unforgiving, I understood that all my homeboys thought I was weak. That's why Rod's words meant so much to me. To hear this man tell me that he was proud of me, respected my decisions and for me to keep doing what I was doing. And when I left that night, I knew I had told him thank you, but I never told him how much that meant to me. I just thought I would tell him next time I saw him. Never thinking there wouldn't be a next time. So, Rod, I know your body can't hear me, but I hope your spirit can. You made me realize that sometimes the streets do forgive, and it also gave me a real family."

There wasn't a dry eye in the chapel. The young men stood, clapped and woofed. Kalissa let her tears run freely, not just from Duke's words but also seeing Rod's smile with that gold shining. She knew he would have been puffed up and so happy to hear the words that flowed from Duke's mouth.

Kalissa felt a hand on her shoulder; it was Fefe. Leaning her head back, Fefe whispered in her ear, "I got goosebumps. He took us to church, sis. Fa real, fa real."

Kalissa nodded, still wiping tears. Nigel grabbed her and buried his head in her shoulder while she did the same.

Duke had stepped away, but he came back and leaned into the microphone.

"One last thing. We got to stop killing one another. We all understand each other's pain without causing more. Let's stop looking at each other as the enemy. We got enough of them already. Peace." Duke stepped down from the pulpit, wiping his face again.

Nigel pulled himself together after the service as they mingled with the family and other people. Rollo walked up to them, and he grabbed Nigel in a bear hug. Then he turned to Kalissa and hugged her the same.

"Mane, this one was hard. You know Rod was my boy from way back." He looked at Kalissa. "Yo' boy talked some good shit today, but if I ever find out who did this shit—" He left it hanging there.

"That's on everythang, my nigga," Nigel dapped him up.

Rollo turned and looked at Kalissa. Her only answer was a small shrug.

Rod's mom called for Nigel to come to the car she stood at. Kalissa rolled her eyes as he walked away. When Rollo started to go in the same direction, she grabbed his arm.

"Hey, Nigel and I need to talk to you soon. Just whenever you have time," Lissa said quietly.

Rollo narrowed his eyes. "Everythang alright, lil' sis?"

Kalissa clasped her hands together to keep them still, and kept her face neutral, in case people were watching. "Umm'hmm, just whenever you're free, come by the house."

Rollo seemed to study her face, while he nodded. "You ain't trying to convert me away from the streets, cuz of what I just said?"

With a glance down, she knocked at the tip of her nose before looking up with a slight smile and fire in her eyes. "Do yo' thang, bro."

A burst of laughter escaped from Rollo. "Ahh, lil' sis, I'ma do the damn thang. That's a promise."

A mutual understanding passed between the two before they exchanged nods and parted.

***

After the awful cemetery ceremony, most people gathered at Mary's, a soul food restaurant. Rollo had reserved the entire place for the occasion. Mary's didn't sell alcohol, but Rollo and Nigel made sure it was on deck.

Fefe and Lissa sat with Duke, talking to him.

"Babay, you said a whole mouthful today. All them niggas needed to hear that!" Fefe exclaimed.

"I just spoke my truth. I really wasn't planning on saying so much, but it just came out," Duke said shyly, clearly embarrassed by all the attention he had been receiving.

"That was your soul speaking and you did a good job. I know Rod was smiling down. I could hear him in my head saying, 'That's my boy, right there'," Kalissa said, with a sad laugh.

"You know when Duck got shot, it bothered me. A lot. I was just glad to hear that he made it. Then this happened, kinda the same way. Man, it fucked me up. I mean Rod didn't really have no beef with nobody. It just didn't make no sense." Duke shook his head, leaning back in his chair.

Vehemently, Fefe replied: "Definitely didn't. He was one of the most chill guys I ever met. But you never know, just like wit' Duck that had nothing to do wit' the streets."

"That's true, y'all know niggas and hoes be hating and you don't even know it. Speaking of Duck, where did he go?" Kalissa looked around.

Duck had come to the funeral in his wheelchair. That's how important it was to him.

"Yeah! And I thought he was walking, what was up wit' that wheelchair?" Duke asked.

Fefe swiped her bangs back and leaned across the table. "Rollo took him home, his energy level is still low and he is walking, but he has to take it easy. Today would have been too much for him."

"Listen at you! Know you have been going to them physical therapy appointments. I ain't mad at cha!" Lissa teased.

"You damn right. I'm in with the family now." Fefe straightened her posture and smiled.

After they laughed, Duke turned serious again. "Did they find out who did that to Duck?" He looked from Fefe to Lissa.

"Naw, we still don't know who those lowdown niggas are," Fefe answered immediately, while Lissa looked at her phone.

"Just like with Desi and now Rod. I know we need to stop hurting each other but it ain't fair that they get away wit' it." Duke looked disgusted.

"Duke! Mane, it's so good to see you!" Taj interrupted them. Drunk.

"Tee! What up wit' you?" Duke stood, crossing arms with Taj.

"You got it. I'm jus' trying to make it." Taj grabbed a chair from another table, scrapping the floor as he dragged it to their table and sat down.

"Tee, you need to put that cup down and take yo' butt home," Fefe frowned at him.

"Gurl, what you talm about it. I'm jus' getting started. I'm straight," Tee said, sipping out of the red Solo cup.

"Where's Rayven? I saw her with you earlier," Lissa asked, moving her chair over slightly.

"She over there talking that same shit as Fe. Don't nobody want to hear that shit," Taj slurred, still sipping.

A look of concern crossed Lissa's face. She had never seen Taj messed up like this, and she didn't like it. Rod's death was hard on all of them, but he didn't need to go down this rabbit hole. She glanced around the restaurant in search of Cedric. Somebody needed to be able to talk some sense into Tee. She decided to try.

"Tee, come on, mane. At least let Rayven drive you home. We can't take no more losses," Kalissa implored him.

"You think I'ma let that bitch drive my whip?" Taj laughed meanly.

Kalissa tried to signal him with her eyes, because the main reason she mentioned Rayven was because she was walking up.

"What bitch you talking about, nigga? Cuz I know damn well you ain't talking about me," Rayven's neck rolled as she stood behind him.

Taj's eyes widened and he made an 'O' with his mouth. But then he fired on. "What other bitch would I be talking about? At least I didn't call you a hoe."

"Aw, hell nah! You must got me fucked up. Come on and take me home. You know what? Don't worry about it, I'll find me a way home." Rayven looked mad enough to fight.

"Cool. That's one less stop fo' me," Taj was on a roll.

Rayven looked around the table, clearly embarrassed, then turned and walked away, cursing with each step. "And yo' ass betta not call me when you sober up."

Nigel walked up, looking confused as his eyes followed Rayven. Duke was looking at his phone, with a slight grin, Fefe still looked disgusted and Kalissa rubbed her head, before breaking the silence.

"Tee, go after her. I don't know what's going on with you two, but you was wrong for that," Kalissa told him.

Taj looked at her innocently. "She don't get mad when her homegirls call her bitch, so why she mad at me? I'm jus' trying to fit in."

Unable to stop themselves, everybody burst out laughing.

"Tee, you stupid as hell," Fefe hollered.

Nigel was ready to go, so Lissa stood, but tried one more time with Taj. "You want us to take you home? I can drive yo' car to the crib."

"Lissa, I'm good. I'm not that drunk. I'll get home okay. Thank you, though," Taj answered with a smile.

"Don't worry, Lissa, between me and Duke, we will make sure this nigga get home," Fefe said.

They all hugged, and Kalissa got to Duke. She punched him in the shoulder. "Don't be a stranger. I expect to hear from you soon."

"You know you will," Duke smiled.

C.D. Blue

Chapter Twenty-Eight

Taj looked out his window, trying to be sure Fefe had pulled off. True to her word, she followed him home and sat in the parking lot until he went in. Like he was a child or something. Taj wasn't ready to be in for the night. Cedric had left the repast early with Monique. Rayven wouldn't answer his calls after his little joke, so he decided to go to the club.

Taj made it to the club in one piece and parked in the back, away from other cars to make sure his didn't get any dings. He promised himself he was only going to have one drink and pick up one woman. One and one. Laughing at his own joke, Taj walked in and went straight to the bar. It hadn't gotten that crowded yet, but he saw some prospects on his way in.

After getting his drink, Taj danced a little at the bar when the DJ blared "Shawty" by Plies. He sat down and started looking around for a suitable woman to take to a hotel and dick down. For one night.

Still chuckling, his smile turned into a frown when he noticed Zandra and a bald-head dude sitting at a table. Looking his way.

"Ain't this some shit," Taj mumbled. It crossed his mind to go to their table and start some shit, but he changed his mind.

Once he finished his drinks, he threw a fifty on the bar and decided to leave. Zandra had fucked his whole night up. Killed his high and everything. He glanced her way and threw his hand up at her in a salute.

The urge to piss hit him as soon as he got to his car. Instead of going back in, Taj looked around and stepped to the front of his vehicle. As soon as he zipped his pants up, he heard someone walking up.

"I guess you thought I was just gonna let you slide for killing my brother," a man growled.

Taj looked around, confused, trying to figure out who he was talking to.

"Huh?"

"Nigga, you heard me. You thought you was scot free, didn't you?" the man said again.

"Mane, if you don't get out my face wit' that bullshit," Taj said, getting angry. "You need to get yo' facts straight before you be wit' yo brother."

By the time Taj realized this was the same man that had been with Zandra, he was hit in the face. Taj rubbed his jaw, tasting the blood in his mouth from his teeth scrapping his lip. His punch landed on the guy's side, right in his kidneys. Taj knew he felt it because he bent slightly over. That's when he jabbed him in the jaw.

They went blow for blow until the guy landed an uppercut that knocked Taj down. The man was on top of him in an instant. When Taj saw the glint of steel in his face, all of his survival instincts took over. They tussled over the gun, until Taj somehow managed to tear it away from him. He pulled the trigger.

Pow!

A look of surprise lined the guys face as Taj pushed him off of him. Taj stood over him, ready to shoot him again when he heard a scream.

"Tee! What have you done?" Zandra screamed.

Taj didn't look back, he knew her voice from anybody's. He got into his car and sped off.

The insistent trilling of the phone woke Lissa up out of deep sleep.

"Hello?" Lissa was so sleepy she couldn't see straight to know who was calling.

All she heard was wind noise and a crying babble. Lissa adjusted her eyes and looked at her phone. It was Taj.

"Tee? Slow down, I can't understand you," she said, getting out of the bed. Nigel opened his eyes, rolled them and turned over with his back to her.

"I think I killed him, Lissa! But that nigga was trying to kill me. Aww, man, why didn't I stay at home? Lissa, I ain't no killa, but that nigga was trying to kill me," Taj cried into the phone.

"Hold up! You shot somebody? What the hell are you talking about, Tee? Come on, bruh, tell me you playing," Lissa almost dropped the phone as she walked to the kitchen; her hands were shaking so bad.

She heard Taj gulp, then he slowed down and explained. "I don't know who that nigga was, that's what I'm trying to tell you. I was leaving the club and this nigga just came out of nowhere talm about I killed his brother. We started fighting and he pulled a piece out on me. I was just trying to get him off me. Fuck, mane." Taj yelled.

By this time Lissa had made it to her kitchen table, and her head dropped as she listened to Taj. She hoped she had heard her friend wrong.

"How did he look, Tee? Who was he?" Lissa whispered, hoping Taj would not confirm her fears.

"Tall, bald-headed, hell, I don't know. Some nigga Zandra's ass fucking wit'. Why, Lissa? Why the fuck would he think I killed somebody? I ain't no killa." Taj had started crying again.

Lissa held her head with her free hand, feeling defeated. She thought she had cried all the tears she had at Rod's funeral but one lone tear dribbled down her cheek.

"Lissa? You there?" Taj moaned.

"I'm here. I don't know why he thought that. Where are you?" Lissa answered, looking up as Nigel walked into the kitchen.

"I'm headed to my uncle's. I can't go to prison for this shit, Lissa, I can't," Taj moaned.

"I know, Tee, I know." Kalissa didn't know what to say. Then she thought of something. "Tee? You still got his gun?"

"Yeah, I got it," Taj sounded hopeful. "Maybe they'll see that it's his gun! That will prove that I was just defending myself."

"Hopefully. Just go to James. He'll know what to do. I'ma stay on the line until you get there," Lissa answered gently, still holding her head and with her eyes closed.

"I'm pulling in now. I'll call you back after I talk to him," Taj said.

Once she hung up, she opened her eyes to Nigel standing at the refrigerator and looking at her.

"What the hell happened?" Nigel asked.

"That damn Malachi. Shit!" Lissa yelled, slamming her phone on the table.

Chapter Twenty-Nine
Six Months Later

Papers and supplies laid haphazardly across her den furniture. Kalissa surveyed the mess, trying to organize everything before she started college. Classes didn't actually start until the next month, but she wanted a head start. Plus, Taj's trial would start the next day and she had no idea how long that would last. She just knew she had to be there for him.

The gun hadn't been registered to anybody, so there was no way to prove it belonged to Malachi. Of course, his story was that Taj was jealous and had shot him about Zandra. Lissa rolled her eyes. As if somebody would ever!

Anger at the situation did nothing to assuage her guilt. Taj knew nothing about what happened to Brian. He never even knew much about their relationship, so she couldn't figure out why Malachi targeted Tee. Other than his association with her.

The doorbell interrupted her anger. When she opened the door, there stood the Sheriff.

"Hello, can I help you with something?" Kalissa asked, her heart hammering in her chest.

"Yes, I'm looking for Nigel Willis," the deputy said, dryly.

"He's not here."

After confirming that she was his wife, the deputy left the papers with her. Anger coursed through her body as she skimmed through them. She couldn't call Nigel fast enough.

"Who the fuck is Shatoria?" She started before he even said hello.

"Huh? Baby, what you talking about?" Nigel said, sounding confused.

"Don't you baby me, nigga. You just got some child support papers from a Shatoria Norman. Now do you know who the fuck she is?" Kalissa yelled.

"Aww, hell naw! I ain't never fucked that bitch. Uh, I'll talk to you when I get home." Nigel hung up in her face.

Kalissa spent the rest of the day mad as hell.By the time Nigel made it home, the kids were home too. It took everything she had in her to keep her cool.

As soon as the children got in the bed, she started with him.

"You ready to talk about this immaculate conception? Or nah?" Kalissa glared at him while he watched television.

Nothing on Nigel's body moved but his eyes. "You gonna let me talk? Or just accuse me?"

Clasping her hands in front of her face, Lissa looked thoughtful. "How am I accusing you? That bitch that served them papers is the one accusing you. I just asked a damn question."

"I already told you," was all Nigel said.

"What you told me was that you never fucked her. Or did you mean you never fucked her raw? 'Cause yo' ass was stuttering," Lissa fired back.

"Since you know every damn thing, why I need to say something?" Nigel looked at her crazy.

Kalissa looked at him in amazement. "Nah, I don't know everything, but I do know that ain't no bitch stupid enough to file child support against somebody she's never fucked. You must think I'm crazy."

Once again, only Nigel's eyes moved. "Like I said, I already told yo' ass once and I ain't gonna keep repeating myself."

Kalissa rose and stood in front of him. "You know what? My best friend's trial is tomorrow, I am not about to do this with you tonight." She leaned forward and got in his face. "But you gonna learn one day, to quit fucking wit' me. I promise you that."

Nigel didn't move, and Kalissa stomped back to the room. Angry and hurt at the same time. She locked the bedroom door, and Nigel stayed on the couch all night.

***

Many might not understand the path you take, but you will not be able to take everyone on your journey. Greatness sometimes requires solitude.

Taj's trial lasted a week. Malachi and Zandra got on the stand and lied. They both said that Taj approached them in the club and then followed Malachi out to the car while Zandra was in the bathroom. Malachi had the nerve to come to the courthouse walking with a cane. The most shocking witness was Darius, Kalissa's old co-worker. He got on the stand, lied and said he witnessed Taj confronting them in the club. Lissa shook her head, knowing that Darius had never even been to any club, much less that one.

Lissa shot daggers at all of them while they were on the stand, and when they sat in the audience. If looks could kill, they would have been laid out.

Kalissa went to the trial every day. Nigel accompanied a few days, but since he had started a new job, he couldn't attend every day. Fefe, Cet, Duck and Rollo also came every day, and they all sat right behind the defense table. As much as she hated to admit it, Rayven had gained her respect. She showed up every day as well. Obviously, she had gotten past her anger about his "joke".

Taj put up a good front, but Lissa knew he was scared. Not only had he told her, but she felt his desperation daily. It floated off him in waves.

When it was the defense turn, they called the few people they could find that testified that they saw Taj leave out by himself and had not witnessed any confrontations. One of the witnesses called was the bartender.

By the end of the week, Kalissa was sick with guilt. She knew things didn't look good for Taj. The idea that he was in this mess just because he was her friend tore her apart. The nights were filled with crazy dreams. Not the ones her grandmother showed up in, but vampires and werewolves. She was torn between telling Taj the truth or just to continue praying that everything work out in his favor. She couldn't tell which was the right way.

To come forward with the truth to Taj would be to leave her kids without parents. To leave the lie in place put her best friend's freedom in jeopardy. All thoughts definitely led to her hatred for Malachi and Zandra.

The trill of her phone stopped her thoughts. It was Taj.

"Hey."

"Hey, Lissa, what's up?" Taj said, sounding down.

"Not much. How are you?" Lissa tried to sound upbeat but failed miserably.

"Tired. Ready to get this shit over. Just in case I have to go away, my uncle told me he would keep everything going for me. You know, my place and car. Him and Cet. He talked to some folks he know downtown and they said if that happens, I shouldn't have to do more than five years. Ain't like the nigga dead or nothing." She heard Taj spit.

"Bruh, don't even think like that. All the people who said they didn't see a confrontation should count for something. Don't you think?" Lissa said, her heart breaking.

"Umm, I don't know. I'm just trying to be ready. Look, I ain't gonna hold you. I just wanted to know if you will be there when the jury come back?" Taj's voice sounded hollow.

"And you know it. I'm wit' you every step of the way," Lissa tried to laugh, but it came out sounding as if she was choking.

"I know. I can always count on you." Taj paused. "I just wish that I had stayed my ass at home that night. I also wish that you had thrown Zandra's ass down the stairs and broke that lying bitch's neck." Taj laughed. "I'm just joking about the second part. I swear though I hate that hoe."

"I know. Zandra always been a liar, but to get on the stand and lie like that? That's big even for her. She showed her true colors. As little as I think of her, I never thought she would do that," Lissa said truthfully.

"Me either, sis. A'ight, I love you, Lissa. That's fa real," Taj spoke quickly, his voice full of emotion.

"I love you, too, bruh. On everything." Tears made Lissa's voice crack.

They hung up, and Lissa sat looking at her phone for a long time.

When the jury came back in, everybody raced to the court-house, except Nigel; he couldn't leave in the middle of his shift.

Kalissa sat in between Fefe and Cedric. They held hands as they waited for the verdict.

"In the case of the State of Alabama versus Tajarius Howell, for the charge of aggravated assault with a deadly weapon, we the jury find the defendant guilty as charged."

The air left the room. Kalissa felt tears crowd her eyes. Cet released her hand and stood up.

"That's some bull!" he yelled.

The judge cracked his gavel, and admonished him and the rest of the audience. The jury foreman continued and found Taj guilty of the lessor charge of having an unregistered firearm.

Taj had dropped his head when the first verdict was called. Kalissa reached over and grabbed his shoulder, massaging it.

The judge cracked his gavel again and set the sentencing for two weeks away. Taj turned and gave everybody there for him a hug. He grabbed Lissa and held her tightly.

"Don't forget about me, nigga," he tried to joke.

"Bruh, don't even say that shit. Remember we are forever solid," she cried while her tears drenched his shirt.

"That's a fact," he said before releasing her.

His mom cried so hard her whole body was shaking, along with his sister and younger brother. The entire scene was heart wrenching.

Filing out the courtroom, Lissa stayed behind while Rollo, Cet, Rayven, Duck and Fefe got on an already crowded elevator. Lissa didn't like being that close to people, plus she needed some time to herself. She stood alone as she waited for the next elevator.

Footsteps sounded behind her, but Lissa didn't turn around. The closed elevator doors showed a distorted version of Malachi behind her.

"Well, well. If it isn't Lady Kalissa. I know your friend isn't going to get as much time as he deserves, but I guess as long as he serves some time, that's good enough," Malachi said evilly.

Without turning around, Lissa spoke, "Your unhealthy obsession led you to send an innocent man to prison. I guess that makes you feel big."

The elevator dinged, and four people stepped off. Lissa and Malachi got on.

"Of course, you would say that. He killed my brother thinking he was protecting you. Zandra told me that Taj would move the world for you. You can stop lying now!" Malachi spat angrily.

Shockwaves hit Kalissa. That's why he targeted Taj, Zandra's stupid ass. A fury flowed through her body like she had never felt. In her anger she felt as if she grew seven feet tall.

"I would only feel big if you had gone to prison too. But I'm not through with you yet. You can bank on that."

Lissa saw Malachi smiling through the elevator doors.

The elevator dinged, and she turned to him.

"You damn right we ain't through. You sent an innocent man to prison like it's a game. I'ma show you how it's really played." She leaned closer to him. "But I don't play to win, I play for keeps. I'll be seeing you around."

She walked out, swinging her hips and purse, passing Zandra on the way.

To Be Continued . . .
For the Love of a Boss 3
Coming Soon

Submission Guideline

Submit the first three chapters of your completed manuscript to ldpsubmissions@gmail.com, subject line: Your book's title. The manuscript must be in a .doc file and sent as an attachment. Document should be in Times New Roman, double spaced and in size 12 font. Also, provide your synopsis and full contact information. If sending multiple submissions, they must each be in a separate email.

Have a story but no way to send it electronically? You can still submit to LDP/Ca$h Presents. Send in the first three chapters, written or typed, of your completed manuscript to:

LDP: Submissions Dept
Po Box 944
Stockbridge, Ga 30281

DO NOT send original manuscript. Must be a duplicate.

Provide your synopsis and a cover letter containing your full contact information.

Thanks for considering LDP and Ca$h Presents.

C.D. Blue

198

COKE KINGS V

KING OF THE TRAP III

By **T.J. Edwards**

GORILLAZ IN THE BAY V

3X KRAZY III

De'Kari

THE STREETS ARE CALLING II

Duquie Wilson

KINGPIN KILLAZ IV

STREET KINGS III

PAID IN BLOOD III

CARTEL KILLAZ IV

DOPE GODS III

Hood Rich

SINS OF A HUSTLA II

ASAD

KINGZ OF THE GAME VI

Playa Ray

SLAUGHTER GANG IV

RUTHLESS HEART IV

By Willie Slaughter

FUK SHYT II

By Blakk Diamond

TRAP QUEEN

RICH $AVAGE II

By Troublesome

YAYO V

GHOST MOB II

Stilloan Robinson

CREAM III

C.D. Blue

By Yolanda Moore
SON OF A DOPE FIEND III
HEAVEN GOT A GHETTO II

By Renta
FOREVER GANGSTA II
GLOCKS ON SATIN SHEETS III

By Adrian Dulan
LOYALTY AIN'T PROMISED III

By Keith Williams
THE PRICE YOU PAY FOR LOVE III

By Destiny Skai
I'M NOTHING WITHOUT HIS LOVE II
SINS OF A THUG II
TO THE THUG I LOVED BEFORE II

By Monet Dragun
LIFE OF A SAVAGE IV
MURDA SEASON IV
GANGLAND CARTEL IV
CHI'RAQ GANGSTAS IV
KILLERS ON ELM STREET IV
JACK BOYZ N DA BRONX III
A DOPEBOY'S DREAM II

By **Romell Tukes**
QUIET MONEY IV
EXTENDED CLIP III
THUG LIFE IV

By **Trai'Quan**
THE STREETS MADE ME III

By **Larry D. Wright**

200

IF YOU CROSS ME ONCE II

ANGEL III

By **Anthony Fields**

FRIEND OR FOE III

By **Mimi**

SAVAGE STORMS III

By **Meesha**

THE STREETS WILL NEVER CLOSE II

By K'ajji

IN THE ARM OF HIS BOSS

By Jamila

HARD AND RUTHLESS III

MOB TOWN 251 II

By Von Diesel

LEVELS TO THIS SHYT II

By Ah'Million

MOB TIES III

By SayNoMore

THE LAST OF THE OGS III

Tranay Adams

FOR THE LOVE OF A BOSS III

By C. D. Blue

MOBBED UP II

By King Rio

BRED IN THE GAME II

By S. Allen

KILLA KOUNTY II

By Khufu

Available Now

RESTRAINING ORDER **I & II**
By **CA$H & Coffee**
LOVE KNOWS NO BOUNDARIES **I II & III**
By **Coffee**
RAISED AS A GOON I, II, III & IV
BRED BY THE SLUMS I, II, III
BLAST FOR ME I & II
ROTTEN TO THE CORE I II III
A BRONX TALE I, II, III
DUFFLE BAG CARTEL I II III IV V VI
HEARTLESS GOON I II III IV V
A SAVAGE DOPEBOY I II
DRUG LORDS I II III
CUTTHROAT MAFIA I II
By **Ghost**
LAY IT DOWN **I & II**
LAST OF A DYING BREED I II
BLOOD STAINS OF A SHOTTA I & II III
By **Jamaica**
LOYAL TO THE GAME I II III
LIFE OF SIN I, II III
By **TJ & Jelissa**
BLOODY COMMAS I & II
SKI MASK CARTEL I II & III
KING OF NEW YORK I II,III IV V
RISE TO POWER I II III

COKE KINGS I II III IV

BORN HEARTLESS I II III IV

KING OF THE TRAP I II

By **T.J. Edwards**

IF LOVING HIM IS WRONG…I & II

LOVE ME EVEN WHEN IT HURTS I II III

By **Jelissa**

WHEN THE STREETS CLAP BACK I & II III

THE HEART OF A SAVAGE I II III

By **Jibril Williams**

A DISTINGUISHED THUG STOLE MY HEART I II & III

LOVE SHOULDN'T HURT I II III IV

RENEGADE BOYS I II III IV

PAID IN KARMA I II III

SAVAGE STORMS I II

AN UNFORESEEN LOVE

By **Meesha**

A GANGSTER'S CODE I &, II III

A GANGSTER'S SYN I II III

THE SAVAGE LIFE I II III

CHAINED TO THE STREETS I II III

BLOOD ON THE MONEY I II III

By J-Blunt

PUSH IT TO THE LIMIT

By **Bre' Hayes**

BLOOD OF A BOSS **I, II, III, IV, V**

SHADOWS OF THE GAME

TRAP BASTARD

By **Askari**

THE STREETS BLEED MURDER **I, II & III**

C.D. Blue

THE HEART OF A GANGSTA I II& III

By **Jerry Jackson**

CUM FOR ME I II III IV V VI VII

An **LDP Erotica Collaboration**

BRIDE OF A HUSTLA **I II & II**

THE FETTI GIRLS **I, II& III**

CORRUPTED BY A GANGSTA I, II III, IV

BLINDED BY HIS LOVE

THE PRICE YOU PAY FOR LOVE I II

DOPE GIRL MAGIC I II III

By **Destiny Skai**

WHEN A GOOD GIRL GOES BAD

By **Adrienne**

THE COST OF LOYALTY I II III

By Kweli

A GANGSTER'S REVENGE **I II III & IV**

THE BOSS MAN'S DAUGHTERS I II III IV V

A SAVAGE LOVE **I & II**

BAE BELONGS TO ME I II

A HUSTLER'S DECEIT I, II, III

WHAT BAD BITCHES DO I, II, III

SOUL OF A MONSTER I II III

KILL ZONE

A DOPE BOY'S QUEEN I II

By **Aryanna**

A KINGPIN'S AMBITON

A KINGPIN'S AMBITION **II**

I MURDER FOR THE DOUGH

By **Ambitious**

TRUE SAVAGE I II III IV V VI VII

204

DOPE BOY MAGIC I, II, III

MIDNIGHT CARTEL I II III

CITY OF KINGZ I II

By **Chris Green**

A DOPEBOY'S PRAYER

By **Eddie "Wolf" Lee**

THE KING CARTEL **I, II & III**

By **Frank Gresham**

THESE NIGGAS AIN'T LOYAL **I, II & III**

By **Nikki Tee**

GANGSTA SHYT **I II &III**

By **CATO**

THE ULTIMATE BETRAYAL

By **Phoenix**

BOSS'N UP **I , II & III**

By **Royal Nicole**

I LOVE YOU TO DEATH

By Destiny J

I RIDE FOR MY HITTA

I STILL RIDE FOR MY HITTA

By **Misty Holt**

LOVE & CHASIN' PAPER

By **Qay Crockett**

TO DIE IN VAIN

SINS OF A HUSTLA

By **ASAD**

BROOKLYN HUSTLAZ

By **Boogsy Morina**

BROOKLYN ON LOCK I & II

By **Sonovia**

C.D. Blue

GANGSTA CITY

By **Teddy Duke**

A DRUG KING AND HIS DIAMOND I & II III

A DOPEMAN'S RICHES

HER MAN, MINE'S TOO I, II

CASH MONEY HO'S

THE WIFEY I USED TO BE I II

By **Nicole Goosby**

TRAPHOUSE KING **I II & III**

KINGPIN KILLAZ I II III

STREET KINGS I II

PAID IN BLOOD **I II**

CARTEL KILLAZ I II III

DOPE GODS I II

By **Hood Rich**

LIPSTICK KILLAH **I, II, III**

CRIME OF PASSION I II & III

FRIEND OR FOE I II

By **Mimi**

STEADY MOBBN' **I, II, III**

THE STREETS STAINED MY SOUL I II

By **Marcellus Allen**

WHO SHOT YA **I, II, III**

SON OF A DOPE FIEND I II

HEAVEN GOT A GHETTO

Renta

GORILLAZ IN THE BAY **I II III IV**

TEARS OF A GANGSTA I II

3X KRAZY I II

DE'KARI

For the Love of a Boss 2

TRIGGADALE I II III
Elijah R. Freeman
GOD BLESS THE TRAPPERS I, II, III
THESE SCANDALOUS STREETS I, II, III
FEAR MY GANGSTA I, II, III IV, V
THESE STREETS DON'T LOVE NOBODY I, II
BURY ME A G I, II, III, IV, V
A GANGSTA'S EMPIRE I, II, III, IV
THE DOPEMAN'S BODYGAURD I II
THE REALEST KILLAZ I II III
THE LAST OF THE OGS I II
Tranay Adams
THE STREETS ARE CALLING
Duquie Wilson
MARRIED TO A BOSS… I II III
By Destiny Skai & Chris Green
KINGZ OF THE GAME I II III IV V
Playa Ray
SLAUGHTER GANG I II III
RUTHLESS HEART I II III
By Willie Slaughter
FUK SHYT
By Blakk Diamond
DON'T F#CK WITH MY HEART I II
By Linnea
ADDICTED TO THE DRAMA I II III
IN THE ARM OF HIS BOSS II
By Jamila
YAYO I II III IV
A SHOOTER'S AMBITION I II

C.D. Blue

BRED IN THE GAME
By S. Allen
TRAP GOD I II III
RICH $AVAGE
By Troublesome
FOREVER GANGSTA
GLOCKS ON SATIN SHEETS I II
By Adrian Dulan
TOE TAGZ I II III
LEVELS TO THIS SHYT
By Ah'Million
KINGPIN DREAMS I II III
By Paper Boi Rari
CONFESSIONS OF A GANGSTA I II III
By Nicholas Lock
I'M NOTHING WITHOUT HIS LOVE
SINS OF A THUG
TO THE THUG I LOVED BEFORE
By Monet Dragun
CAUGHT UP IN THE LIFE I II III
By Robert Baptiste
NEW TO THE GAME I II III
MONEY, MURDER & MEMORIES I II III
By **Malik D. Rice**
LIFE OF A SAVAGE I II III
A GANGSTA'S QUR'AN I II III
MURDA SEASON I II III
GANGLAND CARTEL I II III
CHI'RAQ GANGSTAS I II III

KILLERS ON ELM STREET I II III

JACK BOYZ N DA BRONX I II

A DOPEBOY'S DREAM

By **Romell Tukes**

LOYALTY AIN'T PROMISED I II

By Keith Williams

QUIET MONEY I II III

THUG LIFE I II III

EXTENDED CLIP I II

By **Trai'Quan**

THE STREETS MADE ME I II

By **Larry D. Wright**

THE ULTIMATE SACRIFICE I, II, III, IV, V, VI

KHADIFI

IF YOU CROSS ME ONCE

ANGEL I II

IN THE BLINK OF AN EYE

By **Anthony Fields**

THE LIFE OF A HOOD STAR

By Ca$h & Rashia Wilson

THE STREETS WILL NEVER CLOSE

By K'ajji

CREAM I II

By Yolanda Moore

NIGHTMARES OF A HUSTLA I II III

By King Dream

CONCRETE KILLA I II

By Kingpen

HARD AND RUTHLESS I II

MOB TOWN 251

C.D. Blue

By Von Diesel
GHOST MOB II
Stilloan Robinson
MOB TIES I II
By SayNoMore
BODYMORE MURDERLAND I II III
By Delmont Player
FOR THE LOVE OF A BOSS I II
By C. D. Blue
MOBBED UP
By King Rio
KILLA KOUNTY
By Khufu

BOOKS BY LDP'S CEO, CA$H

TRUST IN NO MAN

TRUST IN NO MAN 2

TRUST IN NO MAN 3

BONDED BY BLOOD

SHORTY GOT A THUG

THUGS CRY

THUGS CRY 2

THUGS CRY 3

TRUST NO BITCH

TRUST NO BITCH 2

TRUST NO BITCH 3

TIL MY CASKET DROPS

RESTRAINING ORDER

RESTRAINING ORDER 2

IN LOVE WITH A CONVICT

LIFE OF A HOOD STAR

C.D. Blue